CHOPPING MALL

A Novel by
Brian G. Berry

Based on the screenplay by
Jim Wynorski and Steve Mitchell

Encyclopocalypse Publications
www.encyclopocalypse.com

Chopping Mall: The Novelization
Based on the screenplay by Jim Wynorski and Steve Mitchell

Copyright © 2024 by Mark Alan Miller and Shout! Factory, LLC
All rights reserved.

ISBN: 978-1-960721-67-9

Cover Design and Formatting by Sean Duregger
Original Poster and VHS Artwork used by permission
Interior design and formatting by Sean Duregger
Edited by Mark Alan Miller

The characters and events in this book are fictitious. Any similarity to real persons, living, dead or undead is coincidental and not intended by the author.

No part of this book may be reproduced in any form or by any electronic or mechanical means, including information storage and retrieval systems, without permission in writing from the publisher, except by a reviewer who may quote brief passages in a review.

FOREWORD
KELLI MARONEY

Brian G. Berry has written a beautiful homage to *Chopping Mall* with this novelization and it makes a terrific companion piece to the film.

I almost never welcome anyone jumping on the *Chopping Mall* bandwagon, but Berry is so respectful and faithful to our movie—and obviously loves and is a fan of *Chopping Mall*—that he has won me over a bit with his novelization.

Berry is a gifted writer and I feel has done *Chopping Mall* justice in this companion piece and/or stand-alone novel.

I truly appreciate and am thankful for the *Chopping Mall* love.

Kelli Maroney
October 12, 2024

For Roger...

CHOPPING MALL

**Where Shopping
Costs You
an Arm
and a Leg!**

CHAPTER 1

Sneaky Pete, that's what they called him. Six-one, a buck eighty, scrawny, with greasy strands of dark hair over deep-set, slate-gray eyes, he busted into the mall with all the confidence of a seasoned criminal. Hiking to the second level without issue, he pulled to a stop in a nook of grainy shadows, a much-needed reprieve from the opened expanse of the neon-shaded walks that made up much of the Park Plaza Mall interior.

"Can't move an inch without some light on you."

The statement held, as every store in the place, emptied of employees and clients, had their windows crowded with buzzing, neon marquees, and cleverly situated advertisements pasted in the windows; looping glass tubes of luminescence that spilled pools of neon shadows.

"Don't matter. Who's gonna put a stop to me? Barney and his flashlight? I'd like to see that."

Sneaky Pete cracked a grin and sauntered off in easy strides that brought him tiptoeing up to the second level. He strolled on without a care in the world, maybe even wishing he'd run into some fifty-something-year-old man with gray hair and a worn-out uniform, and a foot-long flashlight in a shaky hand.

"Bingo," he smiled.

Just ahead, calling to him was the store he was hunting for. It sat in his sights like a ten-point buck. More of those easy strides took him to the display window. Once he got a gander at all the glittering jewelry, he shucked the .44 from his sweater pocket and—CRASH—the window shattered into dust by the rubber-banded butt. Another whack cleared away some of the sharper shards, and he was hands in, grabbing up everything he could and stuffing his pockets until they bulged uncomfortably, which was perfectly fine with Sneaky Pete.

He never did mind some discomfort when money was involved.

Just then, a whirring, mechanical sound came from somewhere nearby. It was an unsettling, mechanical, buzzing drone. "STOP RIGHT THERE."

The pistol was back in Pete's hand without thought, and he spun on his heel, bringing that big .44 bore in line with a...

"What the hell is this?"

"STOP AND SURRENDER YOUR WEAPON."

Sneaky Pete laughed. Was he really seeing this: a robot? Like one of those terror-bots you might see in some 1950s science-fiction film. Squat, a body of heavy alloy, sleek in design, created with durability in mind, it motored along with caterpillar-like treads. It had arms, and the end of which were two pincer-like grip, similar to a crab's claw.

The robot was dark silver, almost metallic-black in color, it had something like a head topping a blunt, conical neck. Flattened almost, it had a red visor where its eyes should have been. Completing this bizarre design was a small yellow box light capped on the top right side of its head.

"You gotta be shitting me." Sneaky Pete stood his ground by extending his .44 man-killer and emptying three chambers in quick succession. His brashness wilted when the slugs that should have put holes in the robot simply ricocheted into sparks.

Lowering the pistol, gunpowder in his face, his morale plummeting, Pete staggered in confusion. The robot's red visor supercharged to a hot neon. Sneaky Pete swung around to make his retreat.

He could hear the robot behind him, gears whirring violently, the treads spinning, the clacking sounds of its pincers promising a bad time. A glance over his shoulder, and he saw the robot was gaining on him. Pete nearly went down on his face as he crashed into a cardboard caricature of some shop's advertising logo.

"*STOP!*"

The voice went up his spine like a skill-saw, sharp and piercing to his brain.

Sneaky Pete tossed his arms in the sky as a probe of needles emerged from the robot, and flew at him, piercing his clothing, and penetrating his skin. He cried like a shot dog and fell, face slamming to the ground, cracking his chin, busting teeth, and spitting blood.

A charge of high voltage pulsed through his body and each wave brought about a spasm that pumped out blood and loops of saliva and foam. Smoke rose off his back and limbs, and eventually, he stopped moving altogether, lying there like something clipped of its strings.

The robot pulled alongside its victim. A tangle of wires hung from its convex belly, tethered to Sneaky Pete's inert, crisping body. Its pincers clacked, and a triumphant soundtrack suddenly swelled.

Words appeared across the screen in bold, blocky yellow letters:

THE END
A SECURE-TRONICS PRODUCTION

CHAPTER 2

The short film left a handful of the audience members watching it in hushed conversations with one another. The projection screen went blank as the movie ended, and the lights in the mall went up. A woman, in her late twenties, popped out of the front row and walked to the platform overlooking the crowd. She wore a beige blazer over a peach top, and a matching skirt. Her blonde hair was yanked into an impeccable bun with feathery bangs hanging over sea-blue eyes. A name tag pinned above her left breast identified her as Miss Vanders.

She smiled and said, "Ladies and gentlemen, that concludes the film portion of our presentation. Now, I'm sure you have questions, so let me introduce you to the Head of Development for Secure-Tronics Unlimited, Dr. Stan Simon."

She clapped along with the crowd as a tall, handsome man with brown feathered hair sprung to the dais in a practiced waltz. Blue blazer, a collared white shirt with a blue tie, and gray slacks, the man had a self-assured smirk plastered on his face as he addressed the audience.

"Thank you very much," he said, his voice deep, resonant. "Before I open the floor, I'd like you all to meet...your brand-new security team." Two women, extravagantly dressed for the occasion, dolled up with voluminous hair and pounds of makeup, emerged from seemingly out of thin air, and removed a sheet concealing the so-called security team that had been hiding on the platform.

The audience gasped.

Three machines, each a carbon copy of the one that apprehended Sneaky Pete in the film, were parked on the dais, shouldered together like troops marching in a parade.

Doctor Simon said, "Say hello to the Protector 101 Series robots. All of Park Plaza Mall's employees have now been trained to work with them."

The audience studied the three robots.

There was a coldness to their design, a ruthlessness, as if these weren't simple security droids intended for mall policy, but something constructed for battle. Some of the attendees in the crowd were noticeably shaken by the presence of the bots. But a man and woman in the front row weren't so easily impressed.

The woman—Mary—was tall, with short blonde hair and deep-set cheekbones. She turned to her male friend, Paul, who was bald with a well-trimmed greying beard, and wore a fashionable orange, crushed-velvet suit with a checkered bowtie.

"Paul," said Mary, "They look like the three stooges."

"Effective immediately," Dr. Simon continued, speaking over the murmuring of the audience, "the Protectors will begin their patrol of the mall—each assigned to one of the three shopping levels."

"I don't know, Mary," said Paul. "The one in the middle has an unpleasantly *ethnic* quality."

"Now, are there any questions?" Dr. Simon asked.

From a few rows back, a man raised out of his seat, his face scrunched up. Miss Vanders smiled: "Yes, Dr. Carrington?"

Dr. Carrington pointed at the three machines in an almost

accusatory fashion. "So what do your *machines* there do besides kill criminals?"

Dr. Simon's answer was well prepared. "Well, first of all, Doctor, the Protectors do not *kill*..."

"Wonder if they kill cockroaches," Mary said, a sardonic smile on her face.

"They could probably be programmed to," Paul replied.

Dr. Simon didn't hear the snide comments. "The Protectors merely detain intruders. They're connected to a computer—" he turned to face the Park Plaza map that was projected behind him "—located on the roof. Using that computer, they remotely patch the mall phone system and send an alarm to the police."

"I don't know. That guy looked awfully dead to me in the video," said the man who asked the first question.

"Just neutralized," Dr. Simon assured him with a salesman's grin. "Protectors can achieve this function in a number of ways. At close range, sleep darts fired from here and here—" he pointed out the areas on the nearest Protector unit, motioning with his finger to its broad, steel-plated breast "—can knock a man out in less than thirty seconds. However, the likelihood of an intruder gaining entry is greatly minimized by the steel security doors positioned in the main exits, which are time-locked from midnight till dawn."

Two thick heavy security doors slid together from the frames of the nearest exit door, and sealed the mall closed with a harsh clanging of locking bolts.

Mary stood up. "Um, they seem so violent," she said. "If they're called *Protectors*, what do they protect?"

"Plenty," Dr. Simon tells her. "For starters, as seen in the film, the Protectors do their work in the mall proper, not in the stores themselves. For instance, lasers positioned here can cut through any sort of debris."

"Maybe I can use them against people I don't like," Paul said to himself.

Another man stood up from his place in the audience. He donned a pressed blazer and slacks off a bargain rack. "Well, that's all very well and good," he said. "But how can your...*things* there distinguish between the good guys and the bad guys?"

Dr. Simon smiled. "That's very simple. Watch." Bringing up a heavy two-way radio the size of a mason brick, he spoke into it. "This is Simon," he said. "Bring number one online."

One of the robots activated and rolled slightly forward. The visor powered on, and was now bright blood-red. A murmur rippled through the crowd as the robot looked around, finally fixing its gaze on Dr. Simon.

The robot spoke. It was the same nightmarish voice from the short film.

"MAY I SEE YOUR IDENTIFICATION BADGE, PLEASE?"

Simon raised his badge an inch away from the visor.

"It's scanning," he told the crowd.

"THANK YOU. HAVE A NICE DAY."

"Same to you," Dr. Simon nodded, lowering his badge.

From his place in the crowd, Paul turned to Mary and said, "It reminds me of your mother. It's the laser eyes."

Simon faced the crowd, waiting for their chatter to peter out.

"There, you see. The system is foolproof. Everyone connected with the mall has been issued an ID badge so when the secure mechanism goes online, the Protectors will make Park Plaza the safest mall in the state."

Paul and Mary regarded each other and rolled their eyes in unison.

"Trust me," Dr. Simon concluded, a smug grin spreading across his face. "Absolutely *nothing* can go wrong."

CHAPTER 3

There wasn't a day that went by during the week that the Park Plaza Mall wasn't teeming with shoppers. There was no escaping the swarms of customers in their bright-colored outfits from head to toe, their shopping bags bulging in both hands, their voices clamoring over the steady flow of pop music blaring over the mall's speaker system. The vast, three-level shopping plaza was the most popular mall in the state.

Closing time was fast approaching. Of course, that did mean there were some stragglers hanging about, getting their last bites of a meal in, or arguing about some price tag put on the wrong merchandise.

Forty more minutes and the stores would close. This pleased Suzie Lynn to no end. She was eager to push her customers out the door and lock up for the evening. She had things to do. Important things. Those important things did not include hanging around in her greasy work clothes and carrying heavy, hot plates to the remnants of the Park Plaza Mall's shoppers.

Suzie Lynn was a petite thing, short, and poster-pretty. Hyper, and unaware of the word shy, she had a great smile and piercing blue eyes that could light up the darkest day. She had a wave of blonde hair to her shoulders, usually crimped, but right then in a single braid down her back.

Thankfully, the restaurant she worked in, La Signora In Rosso, was small. One of the smallest in the mall, but also the busiest. She counted the remaining customers as she worked the floor.

Seven.

Not too bad, could be worse. Half of those were licking their fingers ready for the bill, and the other half were looking like they were just settling in for seconds or some after-meal coffee break.

"Forty more minutes, Suzie, you can do this," she whispered to herself.

Tonight was the night she had been looking forward to all week. Party night. Having the party in mind pushed her to double her speed serving the customers, because it meant she would get to spend some real time with her boyfriend, Greg. But there was more to it than that.

Suzie had been trying to get Alison—the newest waitress hired at La Signora In Rosso—to get out of her gloomy mood and hook up with one of Greg's coworkers; a guy named Ferdy. Of *all* the names he could have...

Alison Parks had been nervous about it. She'd told Suzie repeatedly she wasn't much interested in going on a blind date.

But Suzie—pushy, pushy Suzie—was adamant as always, keeping Alison from floundering in the deep end, pinning her in place with the right words and smiles, explaining how this Ferdy guy was so cute and had a lot going for him. Even sprinkling it with how gentlemanly he was, and he was a perfect match—blah, blah, blah.

Carrying around a pot of decaffeinated coffee—her wrist

cuffed in dozens of multi-colored bracelets—Suzie sauntered between tables. She was handing out checks and topping mugs when, from behind the counter, her boss—*and* the head chef—started demanding she hurry the hell over and grab up the food from the counter that was starting to get cold.

"Come on. Come on, sweetheart!" he bellowed in a thick, Italian accent. His gruff, grimy face was greased in a slick of sweat, and pieces of deli meat were stuck to his chin and embedded in his teeth.

Alison came racing up to the counter, fumbling with a pad of paper in her apron, struggling to get it into her hand. Alison was the girl-next-door type with a head full of feathery blonde curls bouncing around her shoulders, a cute, round face, and powder blue eyes that were big and wide.

"Give me the order. Give it to me! Give it to me," shouted the chef. "What do you got? Andiamo!"

Alison flipped through the sheets of her notepad, nervously. "Can I get two Uncle Luigi belly-busters, a double anchovy pizza, and an order of garlic logs?"

Suzie pulled a face. "That's so gross! What Mojave brain ordered that crap?"

"Guy over there," Alison said, hooking a thumb over her right shoulder without looking.

Suzie saw a man sitting by himself at a table against the back wall, shoveling a fistful of cheese in his mouth. Plump as a swollen barrel, sweaty as the cook, a belly on him like a fifty-pound bag of dog food, with curly black hair out of style and bifocals, he had a slash of ketchup on his left breast pocket.

Suzie laughed. "Oh, God. I should have known it was that weirdo." She started stacking orders in her hands at the same time the boss plucked something from a plate and fingered it into his mouth. "Play it safe, Alison—serve at arm's length, if you get my drift."

Alison looked over at the customer once more as she grabbed a plate. "Thanks for the advice—"

—Alison screamed, burning her fingers on a plate. She dropped it and it shattered on the floor.

The boss looked at her like maybe he was thinking of firing her on the spot or giving her some knuckles across the chin. "Oh, honey, you're breakin' my heart!" he said, his voice dripping with sarcasm.

Suzie felt bad for her.

She knew Alison had a lot on her mind. She squatted beside her friend who was already picking through the ceramic shards and food around her feet.

"Look, Alison," Suzie said in a comforting voice. "In about an hour, we bail this barbecue stand, and it's good times to the max! Don't let the stress of it get to you."

Alison shook her head the same way she had been shaking it all week. "Suzie, you've got a one-track mind. I already told you. I don't know anybody."

Suzie wouldn't let her bail out of this, not now, not ever. Alison *needed* this. She needed to get out of her parents' house, put herself out there in the world independently, break from her nervous shell, and meet someone. According to Suzie anyway.

"Yeah, but you will after tonight. I'm telling you!"

"That's what I'm afraid of," Alison countered with a roll of her blue eyes.

They finished collecting the glass into a small pile on an empty plate and got to their feet. Suzie stared at her friend. "Hey, would I set you up with a slime dog or something? No way, babe."

"Come on! Come on!" the boss shouted. "Take it while it's hot! While it's hot! Girls, come on!"

They gave each other a smile before grabbing up plates heaped with greasy shit considered food.

"Yeah, all right, all right," Suzie said, scowling.

Alison's barrel-body customer at the back table called out, "Waitress, more butter!"

CHAPTER 4

Nighttime.

Thunder broke, lighting slashed, rain threatened to piss on everything.

Marty was pulling the ember hard on his second cigarette of the past twenty minutes, a newspaper folded over to the crossword puzzle in his hands. Reclining comfortably, he was wearing an ankle-length white lab-technician coat over a pinkish collared shirt and dark slacks. His eyes were framed behind a pair of big-lensed glasses. He stared despondently at the ceiling.

Thunder again, its concussive anger belting the mall. It was beginning to shake him up. Alone in that room stuffed with shadowy corners and electronic beeping and humming, it was grating on him. Banks of computers and eight-foot towers of electronics with orange, red, and yellow lights surrounded him. His office, more like some command-and-control center to launch a missile from, was cluttered with computer screens flashing coding, more lights and a confusing array of buttons without order.

Sitting on his desk was a paper plate crusted with the

remains of a plain donut, and an empty Pixie cup needing a refill of something dark and sugary post-haste.

Paper in hand, he swung around in the chair, his eyes landing with suspicion on the three metal monsters lurking in shadows; the state-of-the-art security robots. He took his focus off the Protector units he was in charge of, and put it on the crossword puzzle in his hand.

A rumbling, shifting, banging sound shook the walls and the ceiling. The computer screens flashed with strange color patterns, strobing off and on as if the whole place was running on some giant battery losing its power.

Then everything went out. Night, night. Just a big black box of darkness. Before Marty could utter a word, everything flicked back on just as it was before.

A quick check of the computers' functions showed him all was working as it should.

Thunder exploded in waves again, and the room shook as if it were tumbling off a high cliff. Everything went ape-shit, the computers screaming, sparks flying, lights flickering—the whole thing was some kinetic outburst. Red warning lights kicked off an alarm bell, and the whole office plunged into a mist of red light. Smoke boiled from the backs of computers and electronic towers, and electric currents like lightning bolts danced around the room, bouncing from the computers to the Protectors, and back again.

Marty was instantly out of his seat. He hopped from one bank of computers to the next, bashing the keys with his fists, slamming the towers, breathing out of control—

Then everything stopped, set back to normal again.

He stood there in mid-pose, frozen in fear. Slowly, he came out of it.

"Just a crazy storm. This is wild."

Still, there was something unnatural about it, and he was

suddenly hesitant to move too fast. Oh so slowly, with a motion akin to someone worried about setting off a bomb with one wrong move, he lowered himself into the chair.

Time passed when he allowed himself to relax. In the emergency, he had dropped his cigarette somewhere. Dumping another out of its pack, he lit up, dragged deeply, and looked over to the Protectors.

All good there, just three silent sentinels awaiting orders like good little soldiers.

Shaking his head, he sighed and spun around to his station, eyes going back to his crossword puzzle.

Without warning, a Protector's claw shot out, and struck him in the throat. His eyes bulged hideously as the claw clamped his Adam's apple and, with a simple jerk, tore his throat out.

CHAPTER 5

Ferdy had put up with a lot of bullshit working at Uncle Sid's appliance store. His arms were, at the moment, weighted down with fabric samples as he came out of the back room struggling to keep his balance in check.

Furniture King was the Park Plaza Mall's only furniture store; the same place he had been working for the last few summers now, and it wasn't a bad job. In fact, it was great, because his Uncle Sid was in charge. Anybody else, it might be a pain in the ass. But Ferdy had it okay. At least, he thought he did. The other employees laughed behind his back because they knew Uncle Sid always piled it on heavy for Ferdy. But, Ferdy didn't see it like that. He did his work, and did it well, without complaint. If he had to take on any extra workload because his uncle said, then so be it.

Ferdy, laden with his fabric samples, stumbled awkwardly through the store.

Young, with short brown hair that had a bounce, soft brown eyes, and big glasses, Ferdy was a shy man.

Ferdy moved into the sales corner where his co-workers Greg and Mike were hanging out.

Chopping Mall

Dropping the fabric samples to a coffee table, he eyed Greg who was sitting behind a maple desk scrawling on some paperwork. Mike was there as usual. And, as usual, wasn't doing a damn thing except looking good and chewing his goddamn gum that he never seemed to lose.

Though Ferdy and Mike weren't friends, there wasn't any animosity either. Mike was more like an asshole big brother to Ferdy.

Self-absorbed, Mike Brennan was a big guy, strong, and built like a linebacker. He got plenty of looks from the women who came into the store. All ages, too. When Ferdy told him to back off or they might suffer some sort of harassment case, Mike laughed and said not to worry; it was a sales angle.

Mike was a handsome young man but had one of the most annoying habits Ferdy had ever seen: that constant gum chewing. He would stroll the store, shooting his phone number to the women, smiling his handsome boy smile, chewing and chewing and chewing and chewing that stupid gum.

It irked Ferdy, but Uncle Sid loved Mike, and there was nothing to be done.

Greg Williams, on the other hand, was a nice, kind young man. Most considered him a gentleman and they were right about that. He was the rising face of the business. He had a face that could pull you in and have you signing checks for shit without batting an eye. Greg was business savvy all the way.

Ferdy hung on Greg like he was a mentor. He took his advice, and it was always good.

Mike looked up at Ferdy, his chin bouncing with his gum like an over-cooked piece of steak. "You're not going to chicken shit on us again tonight, right? We already agreed."

Ferdy's face went to stone, his eyes glaring behind the dark frames of his glasses. "You know, if my Uncle Sid finds out I let

17

you do this, I'm dead. You understand that, right? He trusts me to take care of the store while he's gone."

Mike laughed. "He ain't gonna know diddly shit unless you tell him, and you ain't gonna *tell* him, are ya?"

It was just like Mike to start cranking out the thinly veiled threats. But tonight, Ferdy wasn't having that macho bullshit thrown against him. He was done with his gum-chewing ass.

"Hey, look," Ferdy started, his voice firm. "Don't force me to pull rank here."

Mike feigned hurt by the comment, but all it did really was get him riled up, his muscles constricting and bunching, his jaw swinging. In a mimicry of Ferdy, he said, *"Oh, I'm shaking."*

Greg, seeing where this was going, intervened with logic before things got out of hand. "Mike, you're becoming a real candidate for prickhood."

Mike cocked his head to the side like a dog disciplined by his master, a lopsided grin on his face. "What? What did I do?"

"Look, guys," Greg said, ignoring the question. "This party is going to happen, but we need a little teamwork, okay? Besides, if the place looks like shit on Monday, it's *all* our asses, not just yours Ferdy." Greg pointed to Mike, looking him dead in the eyes. "You got plenty of beer, right?"

Mike looked like maybe it was the most stupid question he'd ever been asked in his life. Though not the legal age by far, Mike could get anything just from his good looks alone.

"Greg, come on." He smiled a smile that would melt the panties off any woman. "The fridge is packed! Six cases!"

Greg liked that answer. "All right, good." He sat back in his chair, business-like in tone and expression, addressing people under him as a seasoned leader. "Rick and Linda are bringing the food and some extra brew. Clean sheets are plentiful around here. And, uh, Ferdy? Suzie has a surprise for you."

Mike giggled knowingly.

Chopping Mall

Ferdy blanched. A surprise. No doubt, it was a woman, something Greg had been hinting at all week. Ferdy wasn't up for a date tonight, especially a blind one with a girl he knew nothing about.

Ferdy wasn't a man who dated on a regular basis. Hell, his last relationship was back when his face was peppered with acne in middle school. His nerves were spiking. "I don't know, guys. What if Uncle Sid comes back to the store when we're partying?"

Mike tried goading him with a low, mocking voice, getting his hooks into him. "Come on, Ferdy. Forget about your Uncle Sid for a while. This is gonna work, okay? You'll see."

Greg said, "Ferdy, you can't back out on us now. We made a deal. You must honor that deal. It's how things work."

Ferdy saw no way out of this. Besides, as Greg said, if the place was a shambles come Monday, it would be *all* their asses, not just his. And if came down to it, Ferdy could probably work an angle that would place the blame squarely on Mike.

"Okay, okay, let's party," Ferdy said.

Greg flashed him a smile worthy of a Double-Mint gum commercial. "All right! Good stuff, Ferdy."

CHAPTER 6

A storm had swept into the city. The sky was a battlefield, black and limitless, a sounding board of elemental death, exploding with lightning that slashed the land with electric-blue swords.

Rick wasn't liking it. Stuck beneath the hood of his '82 Bronco, he shook his head. Two miles into the six-mile trip to the mall, and his truck sort of bucked and heaved and went 'putt, putt, putt' and then rolled to a stop like a boulder resting at the bottom of a hill. And like that boulder, it wasn't moving.

Rick was pissed.

Forcing the torque wrench on a bolt, he felt it give and said: "Okay, hun, give it a try!"

Rick's wife, Linda, was in the Bronco's driver's seat. She turned the key, amusing Rick with a tweak of the ignition. What hit Rick's ears were popping, grinding, and stalling noises.

"Shit!"

"Strike three," Linda said, leaning her thick black curls out the window, her smile was wide and perfect, her eyes bright pools of lavender in the storm. "You're out." She'd had enough. She popped her belt and opened the door. "My turn."

Rick, wanting to show his wife that he could perform just as well as she always did, said, "It's okay. I got it. I *got* it."

But when she came up to him, she ruffled his shirt lapels and said, "You know the rules, buster. Into the cab."

He relented with a strained sigh. "Okay, *Butch*. You know I can't resist it when you get tough with me."

She turned away from him as he got behind the wheel. "Yeah, yeah, yeah," she said, still smiling. "Just crank it when I tell ya."

Comfortable in the Bronco, he peeked around the hood and saw his wife's ass poking out in her blue jeans so flush to the skin it dipped deeply between her cheeks. He could never get enough of her, and that body.

Under the hood, Linda tweaked all the things Rick had missed or fucked up. She laid the wrench aside and came out from beneath the hood, all smiles and flashing eyes. "All right. Hit it."

Rick cranked the engine over, frowning in defeat as it purred to life like nothing was ever wrong with it in the first place.

"Always the first time," he said bitterly.

She slammed the hood shut, pumped her fist as she came around the passenger side of the truck, and jumped inside. She saw right away that look of annoyance flush on her husband's face. "I don't want to hear it," she said playfully. "Not another *word*."

"*Me?*" he said, turning to face her. "No way. I covered this whole deal when I said, 'For better or worse' remember?"

She leaned over to him. "Course I remember, I mean, who could forget that stain right there on your tux?"

He was lost in her eyes, feeling himself go to rubber all over again. "Should have been '*for better or weird.*' And speaking of weird, what about this furniture store thing—"

"We haven't had any fun since we sunk all our wedding money into the business. Besides, Suzie's counting on us."

"Honey, I don't care about—"

"Okay. Okay, okay. I guess I won't be needing this," she said, bringing up a lacy white bra and panties in a plush ball and tossing them into his hands with a flick of her fingertips.

He looked down at the lacy stitchwork, feeling a bulge scrape against his zipper.

"Or, um…"

He dropped the panties and bra, put the truck into gear, and slammed on the accelerator with a heavy foot. The Bronco's tires screeched on the pavement as they took off—took off beneath a lightning-streaked sky.

CHAPTER 7

"Attention, shoppers, Park Plaza will be closed in twenty minutes. The mall will be closing in twenty minutes. The lower parking levels will be closed at 10:00pm."

There it went again, the same tired old loop squawked through the Plaza's speaker system every night.

Leslie Todd, huge breasts, blonde hair, thick lips, and pretty green eyes, was engaged in one of her nightly duties at her father's store: folding jeans in nice, neat little piles.

She couldn't stop thinking about it. It consumed her. To think they were actually going to stay after the mall's closing hours to have a party in a furniture store. There was something about it that got her excited. Sex with Mike excited her too, and she couldn't wait.

Mike...her eyes lit up thinking about him. He was her boyfriend now going on six months. They were all about each other in a purely carnal way.

She met him back in the food court one evening. Feeling shy to approach him, he sauntered over, his smile beaming, jawing a pinch of gum. He hit her with his eyes, and she melted. Yep,

Mike Brennan had her vectored and pulled right into him in no time. That same night, they were screwing for hours.

As Leslie let her thoughts about Mike warm her thighs, a pair of rough hands came around and cupped her breasts, squeezing her nipples right through the black silk top she was wearing. She gasped and spun. Seeing Mike, she turned that gasp into a moan. She kissed him and said, "You horny bastard."

Mike chuckled, hooking her against his body and putting one hand on her breast.

"Can't you wait, Brennan?"

"No. No, I can't," he laughed.

How could she resist him? There was no fight in her. Nothing she could offer in the way of defense. He had too much raw sexuality pumping through him. It went through him like high-voltage lines through a transformer. Every touch of his finger, his lips, and...other parts, filled her with quivers.

She laughed playfully as he kissed her lips and neck.

A powerful voice broke in: "What can't you wait for, Michael?"

Mike detached from Leslie like she was a nightmare. Mike saw the man who spoke to him: Leslie's dad. He had eyes that went black and deep, and his face weathered over like a slab of concrete. Wiping the lipstick off his face, Mike fought to control his wits.

"Mr. Todd. Uh, well, I—I—I was just telling Leslie here that, uh, uh—"

Mr. Todd liked Michael as much as he liked men fondling his daughter in his own store, disrespecting him right in his own goddamn place of business.

Leslie took the lead and hooked Mike around the elbow like she was ready to walk the aisle with him, giving her father a voice that was sure to soften the look on his face.

"Daddy," she stressed like a little girl. "He was just telling me how he couldn't wait to take me over to Suzie's house tonight for her, um, birthday party."

Mike nodded in agreement, his smile a mile wide and chomping on a stick of red cinnamon gum. Leslie laid her head on his shoulder like it was all so innocent and natural, and that her dad misconstrued it all.

Crossing his arms, his face screwed up tight, Mr. Todd said, "I see. Well, I'm running late. You'll lock up."

"Sure, I'll take care of *everything*."

"Yes," he said, his glare a seething blade directed at Michael's throat.

All Mike could do was smile back as Mr. Todd stalked off.

"That was a close one," Mike said, wiping his brow.

CHAPTER 8

Alison couldn't believe she had to lie to her father. Never in her life had she lied to her dad, and to think she was doing it for a party of all things. A party. Something she was being forced to do!

But she did it. Yes, she did, and did she feel good about it? Not at all. Everything about it was so wrong, so against who she was and what she stood for. She wanted to vomit.

It was Suzie's fault. That's what it was. Suzie made her do this, forced this into place, and now Alison had to live with it. Suzie wasn't a bad person, and Alison appreciated what she was trying to do for her.

Alison tried looking at it from different angles. She came to the conclusion that, in the end, it was all harmless.

Think about it, she told herself. *It's just a small gathering of some mall employees having a little party. It's not supposed to last all night.* And she could take a taxi home, and her father would never know a thing. It could work! She just had to be careful.

She and Suzie were in the employees locker room, changing out of their work clothes.

"So, what'd he say when you told him?" Suzie asked.

Alison dropped down beside Suzie on a bench. "He said, 'Go out, and have a good time'."

Suzie's excitement came out with a bright smile. She hugged Alison. "Oh, all *right*! That is bitchin'!" She came away from the hug, eyes glittering. "Boy, I wish I had it that easy. My parents still think I'm a kid."

Alison rolled her eyes. "Why do I have the feeling I'm gonna regret this in the morning?"

Waving a comb in Alison's face, Suzie said, "You've had yourself a very rough first week. You owe yourself a little blowout. It'll be fun. I promise you'll have the best time!"

With the sweater knotted around her shoulders, Suzie tied off the sleeves against her chest and forced a weak smile. "Okay, just so long as I don't have to look at any more pizza or garlic logs, I'll be good."

Excited by Alison's approval, Suzie couldn't contain herself. She wrapped Alison in another hug. "Oh, you won't regret this! This is gonna be wonderful!"

"I am still so nervous," Alison said.

"Hairspray, my lovely friend," Suzie demanded, placing her hand out.

Removing the can from her purse, Alison complied. "I really hate blind dates, you know? I went on one last year, and you wouldn't believe how this guy treated me. If he wasn't looking at my breasts, he was checking out my ass…"

Lost in her own world, Suzie looked into her pocket mirror as she sprayed her hair in places. "Oh, yeah! Bodacious. Much better! Lipstick please."

With another dip into her purse, Alison came out with a stick of lipstick. She took the hairspray back. "Suzie—"

"Oh, no," Suzie pouted after seeing the color she was given. "This is a terrible shade. Do you have another color on you?"

"What if he's not my type?" Alison asked, more to herself

than to Suzie by that point. "I don't know how I'll react. What if he doesn't like me? What if he looks at my tits all night?"

Suzie applied the lipstick and smacked her lips, "Oh, yeah, that's it. *Luscious Lust*."

"Suzie, are you even listening? What are we gonna do all night?"

Suzie, pocketed the mirror and lipstick. "Will you stop worrying? Like I said, he's got…"

"*A great personality*," they said together.

"That's right!" Suzie smiled.

"Right."

"He does. You're going to love him. Trust me on this."

Alison wasn't sure what Suzie was basing that on. As far as Alison understood, Suzie had just heard about Ferdy from Greg. She hadn't actually met the guy. He could be a slimeball. Or worse.

They exited the locker rooms and hopped onto the escalator. It took them to the next level.

"Let me see something," Suzie said, flicking Alison's bangs.

"What? What's wrong?"

Suzie brushed away what was bothering her and said, "Finished! You look amazing!"

"Really?"

"Yes, really!"

"Are you sure?"

"Yes, I'm sure!"

"*Really?*"

Suzie hooked Alison by the elbow and rushed away to the entrance of Furniture King with both of them giggling.

CHAPTER 9

Outside the Park Plaza Mall, the bombastic storm was still going strong; a bombing of cosmic, nuclear-blue lightning and an onslaught of biting rain power.

Nessler had escaped the worst of it, ducking into the mall just as the rain blasted in behind him, showering the building wet. Nessler was behind schedule, late for his shift. He was supposed to arrive thirty minutes earlier to relieve Marty for the night.

Tall, thin, and nothing to look at for long, Nessler was your standard-issue cardboard cutout of a scientist. Dressed in the same fashion Marty wore, they both donned big-framed glasses.

He made his way through the mall and finally pushed his way into the office. "Marty," he said. "I'm sorry I'm late, but it was an all-you-could-eat night down at the Pit, and I couldn't resist the opportunity to pig out, you know?"

Marty was nowhere to be found. The back of his chair was facing the control panel as if Marty had simply left his post and hadn't returned yet.

Nessler raised an eyebrow. "Marty?" A quick search of the office showed him it was empty. Everything was running as usual, so that was good. But the absence of Marty was a big no-no. A violation that could cost the man his job, if not *both* of their jobs on account Nessler was late for his shift. The two of them were under strict orders not to abandon the office without another technician present.

"Yo, Marty!" Nessler said again. As he spoke, he nodded a greeting to the Protectors. "How's it hanging guys? A little stiff, I see."

Setting his bag of leftovers on the table, he folded his book in his hand and saw the donut left behind. "Least he could do was clean up after himself."

Nessler's stomach growled. Not one to pass up on his sweets, Nessler plucked it from the plate, gave a look around the office another time, and crammed that crusty quarter chunk into his mouth, swallowing it down.

"Waste not, want not. You know what I mean?" he said, his mouth full, his question directed at the three silent sentinels. "No, I—I guess you wouldn't understand."

Seating himself, Nessler squished along until his rear-end was comfortable. He kicked his feet up on the desk, picking up a book. The book was one of those cheap horror paperbacks, something he picked up at the supermarket early that day. A book called They Came From Outer Space, which was a collection of short stories edited by filmmaker Jim Wynorski.

The first story Nessler had read was called "The Racer," which was a powerful satire that focused on how society glorifies violence for entertainment, especially through media. The story had apparently inspired a film called *Death Race 2000*.

Nessler made a mental note to watch the film. If it was half as crazy as the short story, it was sure to be a wild ride.

Just as Nessler cracked the book open, the sound of a low hum caught his attention.

He turned around, but all he saw were the Protectors huddled over against the wall, shadows at their flanks.

But, something wasn't right.

There was a noticeable change about the Protectors. Some change to their positioning, maybe; he couldn't be sure. But it *was* something. Shaking his head, he went back to his book. He was three words in when he swung back around, sensing something, a chill closing over him.

Again, nothing was there. Just the Protectors.

"Marty, are you here? *Marty?* Hello?"

Nessler again went back to his book. This time, he was nearly a chapter in when the sound of metal sliding over metal froze him in place.

To his back, the Protector rolled several inches, coming to a stop, a panel the size of a baseball card slid open on its breast. Something slid out of the slot. It looked like a wall plug, but pronged with nasty sharp needles.

The phone rang like a klaxon in Nessler's ears, and he sprung straight up, nearly pissing his pants at the sound.

He scooped the phone off its cradle. "Hello, hello? What do you mean, '*who is this?*' You called *me!* No, Marty's not here right —" the caller hung up. Slamming the phone down, Nessler said: "What a damn jerk!"

That's when the needle-tipped prong shot out from the Protector's chamber, launching with a coil of cables, and caught the back of Nessler's neck. It hooked into him and shot out waves of high voltage.

Nessler's body shook and spasmed. The crusty donut re-emerged and flew from his mouth, as did his eyes, popping from his skull, spraying blood. His mouth was jacked open with pain, but he couldn't scream as blood boiled up his throat and pumped from his mouth in a steady, steaming river. Sparks jumped off his body.

A yank of the prong pulled him stiff, and with a little extra pull, the Protector tore his spine out, leaving only an inverted chasm, smoking and dripping blood.

CHAPTER 10

Six-inch speakers blasted tunes out of the boom box, throwing out a pop, dance beat across the store. There wasn't a space in Furniture King to escape its waves. Linda and Rick were pressed into each other, dancing, both popping the caps on their fourth beer of the night.

Work had infiltrated every quarter of their lives and tonight they were rebelling against its advance, attacking with happiness.

For now, work and its pain took the back burner, as the fun and party took the front.

"Happy motoring," Linda said.

"You're so sentimental," Rick smiled, pulling her in for a kiss.

* * *

Locked away in the store's only bathroom, Ferdy stared at himself in the mirror. He could hear everyone out there in Furniture King partying, swinging around, laughing drunkenly.

Ferdy leaned forward to get a better look at himself. Cupping his hand to his mouth, he exhaled, smelling his breath. He needed a mint.

Alison Parks, that was her name. He was thinking about her. She was out there waiting for him. Maybe if he spent all night in the bathroom, he wouldn't have to see or meet her. He could say his stomach was aching and leave it at that.

"Come on, you can do this," he said into the mirror.

Really, he wanted to stay in the bathroom until the party ended, but he knew Greg or Mike would come in there and drag him out. Checking the mirror again, he sighed and took the collar of his white shirt and hiked it, imitating some cool guy look, something he wasn't even close to. And that's why he immediately folded it back into place and shook his head. He wasn't cool, but maybe if he just fixed his hair... "Okay, Ferdy, it's time to be a man and show Alison who you are—"

With a loud bang, Suzie and Greg burst into the bathroom like a commando team and dragged a whining Ferdy through the opening, their hands locked around his elbows.

"Come on, you guys," Ferdy continued whining. "Give me a break. I got a lot of bookkeeping to catch up on. I won't have any time to do it if I party."

"Ferdy, it can wait, man." Greg said. "Stop worrying so much!"

"Yeah. Tonight, you are gonna shake that ultra-Wally image of yours once and for all," Suzie said, removing his glasses from his face and folding them down into his shirt pocket.

"But I like my image. I don't wanna shake it. I am who I am." He placed the glasses back on his face, and said, "Look, you guys just have your fun. I'll clean up when it's over—"

Greg's hands clamped onto Ferdy's shoulders and there was no escape. Greg's grip was too strong. "Look, this is not a democracy. You have no choice in the matter."

Chopping Mall

"But I got a lot of bookkeeping to catch up on like I explained! Uncle Sid will not be happy about this!"

"But *nothing!*" Suzie shouted in his face, dragging him harshly through the store by his elbow. Forcing him to walk in front of her, Greg backing her position, she had Ferdy by the shoulders and made him stand to face Alison.

Ferdy's heart sped up as the smell of Alison's perfume filled his nose. God, she smelled so good. Like some sort of vanilla cookie or something. Maybe a field of vanilla flowers. She smelled amazing. She was way too beautiful for him.

"Ferdy Meisel, meet Alison Parks," Suzie said.

Alison spun around in the chair like something out of a dream, her blue eyes flashing, a smile spreading her red lips open. "Hi."

"Hi," he said to her, all too aware of the big goofy grin on his face.

They seemed to smile at one another for what seemed a long, long time, taking each other's details in.

Suzie softly stepped back to Greg and turned to him. In a soft whisper, she said, "Hi."

Greg smiled down at her. "Hi."

More schoolgirl-like in her delivery, Suzie said, "Hi!"

Greg reached out for her, pulling her firmly against him. "Hi."

Her face became a lustful, craving mask as she wrapped her arms around his neck. She let out a sensual, "Hhhiii."

Greg was stunned by the sound of her voice, eyes locked open. "Hi."

"*Hhhhiii*," she said again, stressing the word out as she bit his lip softly.

"Oh, hello," Greg managed to say before giving her what she wanted.

***

The Protectors left the office behind—leaving both Marty's and Nessler's corpses too.

"PROTECTOR ONE GOING ONLINE, LEVEL ONE."
"PROTECTOR TWO GOING ONLINE, LEVEL TWO."
"PROTECTOR THREE GOING ONLINE, LEVEL THREE."

The Protector units spread out.

CHAPTER 11

"I can't believe this shit!" Mr. Todd said to himself.

He was outside in the blowing rain and wind, thunder booming explosively, lightning raking open pockets of shadows with blue light. He leaned into the wind and covered his face, slipping into a side entrance of the mall.

"If she thinks she's just gonna stay behind with that loser, she's got something else coming!"

That was his baby girl, and he had to protect her. He found a lookout point between some ferns, their leafy green fan leaves concealing him. He could just go charging into the situation, but he wanted to catch that scumbag with his daughter red-handed. He was on the bottom floor, and there was so much open space between him and the escalators. He would have to move fast to reach his objective. Suddenly, he heard a sound. Something mechanical.

He knew it was the Protector. He'd seen the mall training video. In a panic, he padded his pockets for his ID. Securing it in his hand, he felt relieved that he hadn't forgotten that.

The Protector approached, stopped right where Mr. Todd was

hiding, and turned its inscrutable robot head toward him. He'd been caught.

He would simply show the damn thing his credentials and be done with it.

Stepping out from between the ferns, he smiled down at the Protector. There was low vibration sound, like a cat purring. But this wasn't something nice and cute, rather it was strange and... almost menacing.

"Is this what you need?" Mr. Todd placed his ID to the visor. The Protector shot a bright red pulse toward the ID.

Mr. Todd began back to away, pocketing his ID.

"You got my ID, now get out of here you bucket of bolts. You're cramping my style"

Without warning, the Protector fired a red zap that slashed Mr. Todd's hand off at his wrist. He screamed. Another zap and the laser cooked through his chest.

Red smoke billowing off the wound, Mr. Todd looked down in shock. There was a hole the size of a bowling ball in his chest, and blood and meat were spilling out.

Another red laser light centered itself on Mr. Todd's forehead. His eyes crossed, trying to look at it, then the Protector fired its deadly laser, and Mr. Todd's face and head exploded, spraying viscera like a geyser.

"THANK YOU. HAVE A NICE DAY."

CHAPTER 12

Linda wasted no time whatsoever. She came through the curtain drawn alongside the bed like a mirage, a man's dream and fantasy woven into a miracle emergence. She was everything to Rick. Every hot thought, every wet dream, every boner during the day. She was dressed in a black silk nightgown.

But she wasn't dressed for long. She slid the sleeves off her shoulders, and the gown dripped to the floor like liquid. Seeing Linda standing there in sheer white bra and panties, Rick was beside himself, his erection lifting a tent under the sheet. Her eyes went to the steeple of his erection, and she licked her lips.

"You, uh, you uh, look amazing," he said.

Rick, laying there waiting for her to leap on him, his chest exposed, well-chiseled, burnished copper by the sun, had his hands crossed under his head, a smile spilling on his face. He was seeing Linda like he had never seen her before. Something new was in her eyes, a powerful sexual energy. The heat of it was on him like a fever. The black curls of her hair draped her face a bit, showing him the violet dots of her eyes.

"Lady," he said, laying it thick and suave. "You, uh, got a license for that outfit?"

She brushed a swath of hair over her ear. "Why, uh, no, Officer. I guess you're just gonna have to take me *in*."

She tossed herself at him. Immediately, his arms were locked around her waist, his mouth on hers. She dragged a hand down his chest and abs until her fingers found his erection and wrapped it tight.

"Is this for me?"

He couldn't speak as a moan whispered out of his mouth.

"I guess that's a yes."

* * *

Greg was out of his clothes soon after Suzie put her tongue in his mouth. She had a way to her that made him quiver and melt; he was addicted. They had found a little spot away from the others and made it their own.

"Getting excited I see."

Yes, Greg was more than excited. Suzie felt his hardness pushing against her belly. She was lying on top of him, dragging a finger down his chest, her lips pressing lightly on his neck, kissing and teasing.

Greg smiled. "You smell like pepperoni."

Suzie's smile dropped to a pout, she rolled off of him, getting to her feet and crossing her arms. She was acting as if she were mad at his comment. But she wasn't. It was just one of the little games they liked to play.

"Pepperoni?" She began to walk off, swaying her hips. "Well, if that's the way you feel—"

"Wait a minute," Greg said, his hand snapping to her hip.

Biting her lip, she asked playfully, "What?"

"You didn't let me finish. I *like* pepperoni."

Keeping her stance, her arms crossed, she giggled. "Oh. In that case."

Chopping Mall

With her back to him, she peeled down the leotard straps and her sheer black top until her breasts were exposed. Placing her hands over them, she turned to him, releasing her hold. Greg's eyes lit up like Christmas bulbs, his mouth falling open.

* * *

Mike was having a hell of a time trying to please Leslie. Normally, she wasn't so uptight about things, but something about tonight was digging at her. Mike wasn't sure what that could be, but didn't really care either way. He had one objective in mind, and it was inches from his face, musty and hot.

"*Mike*," she said, rolling her eyes.

"What *now*?" he asked her, his voice muffled beneath the cover as he tried to go down on her.

"You know I don't allow *that*."

He rolled his eyes. "You allowed it last week, didn't you? Huh?" His tongue leaped to her thigh and went up to her breast, circling each nipple until both were hard and erect as gumdrops.

"What are you doing—"

But whatever other complaint she had was shelved as his tongue went into her mouth, and he rammed himself inside of her.

* * *

While everybody was engaged in their amorous activity, Ferdy and Alison were separated from the moans and outbursts of ecstasy.

Seated together on an ugly flower-spotted sofa, they focused their attention on the television sitting on the coffee table in front of them.

The movie was Ferdy's choice. Being a science fiction/horror movie buff, he put on one of his all-time favorites: *Attack of the Crab Monsters*.

Alison's face pinched as she watched a mountain of a crab emerge from a roaring surf, skittering onto the beach. A man in swim trunks and bare chest approached its snapping pincers with a bomb in his hand. He almost made the connection when one pincer whacked him off balance and he flew back, the bomb taking flight and—*BOOM*—blew up harmlessly out of range.

"Ohh!"

Alison hadn't even realized she buried her face in Ferdy's shoulder after the scene.

Ferdy laughed. She smiled back at him. "Heh. Sorry about that. I scare so easily."

Ferdy could have suggested anything to watch, but he decided on a comfort movie, something to relax him and make him feel in control of his emotions. He couldn't imagine watching a romance flick or something comparable. He would be a sweaty, stiff mess, sitting there like a dead thing as Alison watched the film.

Also, the movie's soundtrack and constant monster sounds worked to muffle any sexual noises in the backdrop, so that was a plus.

"I'm sorry. I should have told you about that. I've seen this one a few times." He lied, knowing very well he had seen it hundreds of times. Pausing the movie, he tried to think of something useful to say.

As luck would have it, Ferdy really liked Alison. Liked her a whole lot. He wanted to show her a good time, but he wasn't sure how to go about it.

And, like an idiot, you show her Attack of the Crab Monsters. Good one, Ferdy. "Could I get you some more wine?" he asked, hoping to settle her nerves.

"Ferdy...are you trying to get me drunk?"

Chopping Mall

His eyes widened. Now he was in a spot. What was he thinking asking her if she wanted more wine? Maybe it was the little amount of beer he had. He knew he shouldn't have had any booze, but Greg practically shoved that Pilsner down his throat.

Smart move, you idiot, now she thinks you're just like the rest of those assholes!

He had to find the right words and tread carefully. Any wrong move might end something that could be beautiful down the road. "No, no. I—I just figured maybe you might be thirsty is all." He sighed. "You know, part of the reason why Greg fixed me up here tonight was so I—I wouldn't squeal to my uncle. I never thought that, uh—"

She moved in closer to him, her smile wide. "What?"

Damn, was it hard to speak to a woman. Not just any woman, but a beautiful woman like Alison. It wasn't like speaking to a customer or something.

"I never thought it would be so, uh…you know, *nice*."

"You know, Ferdy, it's…*nice* for me, too—"

"*Oh, God! Oh, God! You're the king, you're the king!*"

—Alison and Ferdy's faces froze, listening to Leslie scream out for Mike's thrusts. They broke up their nervousness with laughter.

"Chalk one up for Furniture King," Ferdy said, trying to be funny.

"Sounds like they're having a nice time," Alison said.

"Yeah. Well…it's getting kind of late. The mall's gonna seal up in about an hour. What do you say I take you home?"

Alison looked at Ferdy like he was the only man in the world. "That's real sweet, Ferdy, but if it's all right with *you*…" Surprising herself, she took her empty cup and flung it over her head. Ferdy watched it sail then land in a waste basket of empty beer cans. "*We* can stay a little while longer."

Ferdy was impressed, not only with the blind toss, but this

girl, Alison. She was everything he had ever wanted in a woman and didn't know it yet. "Nice shot," he said.

She reached out and took his glasses off. She pulled him in with one hand behind his head. They stared at each other, her fingers in his hair. The *Crab Monsters* credits started rolling, and that's when Alison made her move, going in for the kiss.

For one moment, Ferdy thought he might launch out of his pants. Her tongue was warm honey. They melted into each other, hands roving, tongues thrusting, and they didn't stop even when the television turned to static.

CHAPTER 13

Boy, if he could do it all over again, he probably wouldn't have. Walter Paisley didn't have much in the way of smarts. His whole life had been one failure after the next. On the bad side of fifty, face cracked with stress lines, thinning gray hair, eyes sunk in pockets of exhaustion, he worked sixty hours a week at the Park Plaza Mall. He hated every goddamn second of it.

In front of him was a mess worthy of a whole construction site. Some idiot—no doubt one of those dumb-ass kids—left a whole lake of a mess on the floor that was wreaking havoc on his mop heads. This was the third such mop head he'd had to replace. That's how bad it was.

Squishing it in the wringer was leaving an awful mess in the bucket. This was the sixth time he had to empty the bucket in the drain, and *still* there was so much to clean up.

He wished he had a beer right now, maybe a cigarette hanging off his lip. He didn't smoke, not at all, but right then, he would have dragged a whole carton to ash.

Swishing the mop head around, his face soured seeing something like puke and hamburger mixed in with chocolate shake and Chan's noodles-to-go. God, what he wouldn't give to find the culprit behind this bullshit. Thing was, not one of his friends had the courage to help him out. No, they were making fun of him, poking jokes and such.

"Of all the damn nights, a Friday!"

The way he saw it, his timecard should have been punched hours ago. He should be in his favorite chair, his feet kicked up comfortably, six beers into a case, watching the Dodgers smack 'em over center field. But that would have to wait.

Swish, squeeze, repeat. As he worked, laughter echoed over to him. It was Dick and Miller, those sonsofbitches. He knew they had punched out a while ago, sucking down off-work beers. The sound of their heels was coming closer.

He was hoping like hell they would just pass him by without a word, but he knew that was about as likely as him hitting a million on his next scratcher ticket.

"Yo, Walter. You having a good time?" It was Dick.

Shit. Miller was bad, but not as bad as Dick. The man always had some ridiculous nonsense.

Walter chose to ignore the comment and focus on the task, wiping and straining, wiping and straining. Then Miller was suddenly there and had to add *his* two cents.

"Dick, you know Paisley, man. He loves a challenge."

Goddammit. They were standing there, hanging on each other, beers in their hands, their uniforms clean, their faces bright with smiles. Walter couldn't let these two dip shits get away with mocking him.

"Go ahead and laugh, you guys, but if I ever find the bastards that did this, they're dead meat."

Dick dribbled his beer down his chest and laughed. "Right, Walter. Right. Say, you better hustle it up, buddy, you don't wanna get locked up in here again, do you?"

Chopping Mall

Of course Dick had to mention last week's little episode. A week ago, Walter was finishing up some last-minute cleaning in one of the third level bathrooms—a plugged toilet of all things—when the time got away from him, and he ended up spending the night in the mall. A mistake those idiots wouldn't let him live down.

"Hey, rub it in all you like. I'll be out of here in ten minutes. You'll see."

They burst out laughing, slapping each other's back. Walter tightened his grip on the mop handle, thinking of whacking them upside their heads, bashing their balls in. Luckily for them, they had better things to do and ended waltzing out of there before Walter could play out his little fantasy.

"Creeps," he mouthed.

Back to the task. His mop squishing, sliding, straining —*PLOP*—into the bucket. Nasty, nasty, nasty, is what he thought as chunks of things bobbed on the surface in the bucket, while others sank out of sight.

"Bastards." He wished he would have caught the little ankle-biters who made such a mess. He couldn't believe someone could do something like this and leave it without at least reporting it to someone in charge.

Caught up in his anger over the situation, he missed the approach of the Protector unit rolling up at his six. His shoulders working with each swish of the mop, he still hadn't realized it was there until it bumped into the bucket, knocking it over, spilling its contents back out around Walter's ankles.

There was never a face so red in the history of the mall's employee database. Walter swung around, ready to bash someone's brains out, the mop in his hands like some sort of combat staff. His eyes bugged when he saw the culprit was one of those tinker-toy machine robot things.

"You clumsy sonofabitch. Look at what you did! I ought to turn you into scrap metal for this!"

"*MAY I SEE YOUR IDENTIFICATION BADGE, PLEASE?*"

"Identification badge?" Walter asked, annoyed by the question, annoyed by the day, the night, the entire week. He was looking over the robot for a weak spot, a place to land a few blows with the mop staff or maybe crack that visor and let the red light spill out.

"*DO NOT MAKE ANY SUDDEN MOVES.*"

Oh boy, was Walter ever mad now. His ire hiked to the breaking point, blood pressure off the charts, knuckles white on the mop handle, he giggled like some sort of madman and said: "Sudden moves? I'll give you a *sudden* move upside your head!"

The Protector sprung out a bundle of wires that landed in the puddle at Walter's feet.

If he hadn't been so pissed off, he might have laughed until his seams busted. A piece of metal that probably cost the mall a million dollars per unit, had malfunctioned and misfired wires like ten-pound fishing line.

"What the hell is that?" he asked. "What is this you worthless pile of junk, huh?"

The Protector's head cycled left and right.

"Hey, look, I'm like you, you know?" He fingered his ID badge clipped to his left breast pocket. "I work here. See? Huh? *See that?!*"

What a joke, Walter thought. This thing was supposed to scan and move along. But it wasn't doing that at all. It was sitting there, immobile as a block of cement. For the cash the executives of the mall paid for these things, they could have invested in Walter, and he would have gladly walked the mall all night and day. In his way of thinking, machines had no right to replace humans.

Chopping Mall

"I knew you bastards were gonna be trouble when they first brought you—"

Walter screamed as what felt like fifty-thousand volts exploded through his body, attacking every nerve center, streaming through his blood like lava. The Protector had sent an electrical current through the wires, and into the dirty water. Walter's skin started to cook and split and out poured blood black as motor oil, steaming and hissing with each new rip in his body. Sparks sprayed off his joints, his eyes busting to slime behind jets of blue flames. His mouth wrenched open, black smoke boiled out of his throat. In less than thirty seconds, Walter Paisley had completely turned to slop, spreading out in a pool of bloody, heated goo.

The Protector pulled in close to the steaming mire.

"*Thank you. Have a nice day.*"

***

Dick was the first to say: "Did you hear something?"

Miller took another pull off his beer, let it slide down his throat. "Yeah, but who cares?"

Dick had a feeling it was a scream. He dropped his empty bottle into a trash can and turned around. "Sounded like it came from over by Walter."

Miller laughed at that, beer trickling down his chin. "Let's go check it out, I guess."

They came back to the area where Walter had been mopping up, immediately stopping in their tracks, faces stricken with horror.

"What in the shit is that!" Miller said.

Dick tried to answer, but he couldn't wrap his head around it, couldn't find the words. "Is…that…"

Miller dropped his beer. "That—that's *Walter*!"

Dick wouldn't have believed it if he hadn't seen it. But now, there was no way not to see it. Walter was in the mess there... somewhere. They saw a partial rack of bones in the shape of skeleton at least. Not white bones, but blackened, charred, crisped. Ropes of smoke spiraled off the heap. A biological waste zone. They spotted a head off to the side, the crown broken open, the orbital slots cracked and smoking.

"Jesus Christ, Dick! We gotta call the police!"

"I...shit. I can't think."

"It's okay," Miller told him. "Wait right here."

Miller was all set to make the run to the phone booths just a short distance away, but then a cold, mechanical voice spoke to him.

"STOP RIGHT THERE AND SHOW YOUR IDENTIFICATION BADGE."

Immediate relief washed through Miller when he saw the security bot. "Oh, yes, hey, over here!" He dashed over to the Protector and flashed his ID. "Can you call the police? Are you programmed for that?"

The Protector read his ID, and as soon as Miller pocketed it, a laser sliced open his belly and another sank through his face. He couldn't scream or do much of anything other than spin in a circle belching blood and steam. He made a whole big mess, spinning and flinging out loops of blood.

Another laser, and his torso split open, which caused it to snap back and rip off his waist. Blood ejected in high-pressure jets as his legs walked six feet and toppled over, a bucket of blood splashing right out of him.

Dick watched this whole thing go down, and there wasn't anything he could do. He was stuck there, piss rolling down his leg. His bowels released. His eyes never blinked; his breath never came. Before Dick could even gather his thoughts, the Protector turned to face him. The robot didn't even give him time to show his badge. Instead, a laser shot out, piercing Dick's chest, belly, groin, and face.

Pieces of Dick lay in a spreading pool of blood, the bottom half of his jaw sliding away over the mall's floor, the tongue hanging over the teeth.

"Level One, all clear."

CHAPTER 14

One of Leslie's habits Mike was tired of—and there was a big list of them—was her smoking. He couldn't stand smokers, especially the smell of cigarettes. The smell got into everything, embedding itself in the smallest fibers, and it was hell washing it out. Even on the skin, it seemed to permeate individual skin cells, becoming a permanent aroma.

"You know, Leslie, smoking is bad for your health."

She fixed her eyes on him, blinking. "I told you, Mike, I have to have a cigarette. Especially after sex." She took her purse and started rifling through it. When her frustration got the better of her, she dumped out everything onto the blanket covering her stomach. "Shit, I think I'm out!"

Mike rolled to her side. "Are you for real? Can't you think of anything you'd rather have besides a smoke?" His hand went under the blanket until his fingers found her vulva, stroking it softly. Leaning in, he kissed her neck, moving up to her lips.

But she wasn't having it. She shoved his hand away and pulled back from his mouth. "No."

Falling onto his side of the bed, he sighed. Reaching to the floor for his jeans, he pulled out a stick of gum from the pocket and put it in his mouth. Knowing if she didn't get her cigarettes, she would turn the whole mood into something unpleasant, he said, "Okay. Okay. Uh, I think Singleton left a pack of Camels under the register. I can go check for you."

Pouting and crossing her arms like some spoiled brat, she shook her head. "*Camels?* No way. You know I only smoke Virgin Lights—100s preferably."

Unbelievable. Actually, no, this was pretty believable. Leslie was spoiled rotten by her father. Why would he think she would smoke just any old brand of cigarettes, even if they were free?

"What do you expect me to do? Go out in the mall and buy a pack?"

She ran her finger up his chest, circling his pectorals, driving her fingertip under his chin. She leaned into him and smacked a kiss to his cheek. Batting her eyelashes, she looked him square in the eyes. "There's a machine right down by the phones."

Getting out of bed, he started to pull his pants on. "You always get your way, don't you?"

"When *I'm* happy, *everybody's* happy."

Hiking his jeans up, he left them unbuttoned. "That's for sure. Hand me my badge, will you?"

"What's the magic word?"

Gum smacking loudly, he forced a smile and said, "Hand me my badge, *please*."

Staying in the bed, she grabbed the badge off the nightstand and offered it to Mike, holding it out between her fingers.

He took it. "Thaaannnk you."

He started walking when Leslie called to him. "Oh, Mike?"

Turning around, he said, "What, what, *what, what, what?*"

Yanking the cover low to her flat belly, she revealed her perfect breasts, and squeezed them together with her arms, plumping them up, the pink nipples erect.

"Hurry back," she purred.

Jaw hitting the floor, he groaned. "Count on it."

* * *

Barefooted in the mall, that was something new for Mike. If it hadn't been for Leslie and her craving, he wouldn't be footing it down the landing, stores on either side throwing out a carpet of neon shades.

He'd been working in the plaza for a couple of years now, and he had never seen it so dead.

It was nice. Every day the mall was flooded with people and their voices, laughter, and screaming kids. So, to see it completely devoid of customers was almost…eerie.

Alone with his thoughts, he drifted back to memories with Leslie. As much as he was starting to fall for her, he couldn't let himself fall too deep. There were too many women in the world. To be devoted to just one was not right. He needed to spread his wings, sink his anchor into different ports.

He turned into the alcove where the vending machines were stationed. One side was a bank of phones, and across from those, the cigarette machine.

Dipping a hand into his pocket, he fished some coins out, his eye roaming the cigarettes. He found Leslie's brand and squinted at the price. "A buck and a quarter?!"

Reaching back into his pocket, he pulled the additional coins out and stopped. His skin prickled coldly. He had a feeling that he was being watched. So stressful was the feeling, he turned quickly, expecting to see Leslie or maybe Greg or somebody messing with him.

But there was nothing there.

He slotted the coins, and then a noise made him pause. This was a mechanical sound, something rumbling like voltage, like walking past power lines.

"Leslie?" he asked.

He wasn't sure why he thought of her right away. He knew she wouldn't come after him. Leslie Todd? Actually getting out of bed and checking on him? Not likely. He was all set to turn back around when the phone on the wall across from him rang, and he nearly jumped out of his skin.

"Shit!" he said. Sighing, he grabbed the phone. "Hello? What? No, Jamal, there haven't been any messages for you." The phone went dead. He shook his head and hung it back up.

He went back to the cigarette machine again, checked his hair in the silver reflective casing, and pulled the rod on the Virgin Lights—

"MAY I SEE YOUR IDENTIFICATION BADGE, PLEASE?"

Mike jerked back as if someone had physically spun him around. He saw the Protector unit there. "Jeez, you little bastards are weird." He slipped his hand into his pocket to retrieve the ID. "Here. Klaatu Barada Nikt0, okay?"

The Protector's visor lit up. Its computer eyes reading off the bar code. Mike figured it was finished assessing his right to be in the mall. When the visor light dimmed, Mike pocketed his ID, shaking his head again. He took the cigarettes from the dispenser tray, and the Protector's arms sprung out at its side, its pincers clacking wildly. Its visor turned a hot red.

Palms up, backing away, Mike's face fell in confusion. "Hey now, what's going on? I showed you my ID! What are you doing?"

Mike backed into a service door, swung around to make his exit. He took the handle and pumped it. The door was locked. Of course it was, he thought. This whole night was full of traps and disappointments.

That's when a pain hit his back like the blow of a hammer. His body went stiff, and his limbs locked up. He didn't even scream when he toppled to the ground like a store mannequin in an earthquake.

Unable to move or defend himself, all he could do was watch. And watch he did, without screaming, as the pincer sprung at his throat and took hold, sinking its metallic hooks into his throat and ripped away a flap. Blood sprayed and arced over his chest. Next, the claw pinched into his eyes, closed, and ripped his face off.

* * *

Leslie couldn't find her shirt. Mike was taking forever, and she was jonesing for her nicotine hit.

"Damn you, Mike!"

Finding his shirt, she slipped it on and got to her feet.

Naked from the waist down, she found her blue panties and hiked them up, leaving a meaty portion of her ass cheeks hanging out.

Now, she just had to tighten the shirt that was three sizes too large for her little frame. But she managed. Inside Furniture King, the atmosphere was dead. Not bothering to inform anyone she was leaving, she stormed out of there, closing the doors behind her.

She walked a few steps into the mall, looking left and right. "Mike?"

He had to be finished getting her cigarettes by now. He'd been gone for nearly ten minutes. It took a minute or two to walk to the machine down at the end of this walkway, so what was the deal?

"Brennan, you ass. I'm not in the mood for games! If you're hiding out here somewhere, I'm going to kill you!"

Stamping her foot, she marched off to the vending machine, irritation in every step.

Chopping Mall

* * *

Ferdy decided not to put on another horror or science fiction flick, instead, just finding some late-night sitcom on the television to keep them company. Not that they needed it. But it helped to mitigate any unease that was lingering.

Alison had spotted Leslie sneaking out of the store, and she didn't look too happy.

"What is it with those two, anyway?" Alison asked.

Ferdy's arms went up. "Personally, I can't figure it out. All they do is have sex and fight. It's disgusting."

"Like most couples," Alison added with a roll of her eyes.

"Yeah," Ferdy replied uneasily.

"Ferdy…"

"Yeah?"

She slipped her sweater back over her shoulders, feeling comfortable and grateful for such a nice guy. *"Thanks."*

Ferdy smiled. Taking the remote from the table, he clicked the TV off and leaned back next to her. A hundred thoughts ran through his head, and all of them had to do with Alison. She was perfect in every way. And the time they spent together was amazing.

His heart was racing. His emotions spiking. He wanted to kiss her, touch her, hold her. So, in a move shocking to himself, he did just that.

* * *

Leslie was now officially uncomfortable. She was hugging herself, walking slowly through a tide of shadowy walls, neon lights intersecting and making the mall very spooky.

She reached the alcove where the cigarette machine stood. All the lights were off. Something wasn't right here. She could feel it deep in her bones, an almost haunting sensation that latched onto her mind.

"Mike?" There was no reply. No movement. So where could he have gotten off to? The other cigarette machine was on the second level. Maybe he had gone there, considering the lack of lights here. "Mike? Are you there?"

She took a step closer to the cavity of shadows. There was thickness in the air.

"Mike. *Damn* you!"

Another step, her body started tingling with gooseflesh. It ran up and down her arms and legs, pebbling her skin and raising the hairs.

"Brennan, if you don't come out now, don't even bother," she said.

Then she saw legs. Mike's legs.

Now he was going to get it. Leslie was pissed. She crouched, her hands reaching for him. She could see a vague imprint of him hiding in the shadows. "Damnit, Mike, say something!"

She was shaking him now. "Stop fucking with me. You're not sleeping. Wake up! I said wake up! I don't need this shit!" Suddenly, he sprung out at her, his face missing. He was just a grinning, bleeding skull, with bits of meat stuck to the bone, eyes packed with gore, a wave of blood congealing down his chest.

That's when the service doors blew open wide, blue mist pouring out of them. Leslie fell back onto her ass and clawed a retreat, screaming.

It was the Protector unit, curtained in the blue mist, tendrils spilling over its sleek, metallic shell. Its pincers were reaching for her, its red visor bright and pulsing.

Leslie scrambled up and took off, leaving the robot behind, running back to the store.

Pink lasers streaked around her, landing with percussive crashes that sprayed sparks and set walls and patches of carpet on fire. Leslie heard its motor getting closer, gaining on her. The treads spun as its lasers cooked up the mall. Her heart was beating like a fist determined to crack her sternum from the inside.

A single laser slit her hip open, and she felt a white-hot explosion of pain. Her scream echoed. Another laser beam clipped her shoulder, and she staggered. The wound crackled and smoked. She was smoking now, just not the way she'd wanted.

Furniture King was up ahead, its sign glowing brightly, showing her the way to salvation. The Protector was closing in fast. Another pink ray whipped out and stung her ass cheek. A trail of fat and blood bubbled out, leaving sizzling droplets on the mall's floor behind her.

She would make it! She was determined to make it. The store was within reach. The doors were right there, a few feet away. Her friends must have heard her screaming because they were pressed up against the windows now, in various dress.

Their eyes were all glued to the thing behind her. Following their gaze, she turned, seeing the motorized horror revving up to meet her. She let go with one soul-shattering scream as a burst of pink light streaked from the visor and slammed into her face, vaporizing her head in one brilliant Technicolor explosion of brain and blood and bone. Stiff, she dropped to the ground, the stump of her neck boiling and bubbling.

Linda screamed as a splash of blood hit the window, bits of gore dripped down the pane. "Oh my God!"

Ferdy's face turned green.

Greg and Suzie were holding each other, their arms strong around one another. She was crying and shaking and whimpering, her face going white as cream when the window took a spray of blood.

"Oh, God," said Suzie.

"Thank you. Have a nice day."

The Protector swiveled, facing Furniture King and the many intruders standing inside.

"Protector One, arming. Detain intruders."

Linda struggled to see beyond the red window and its many rivulets of blood. Beyond the first Protector, she spotted movement. "Oh, my God, there's another one!"

"Protector Two, arming. Assist Protector One."

Greg moved into action saying, "The storeroom. Quick, let's go."

Now, they were all seeing the Protectors gearing up for a frontal assault. Suzie was pasted to the window in sheer terror. Greg had to pry and peel her away, and finally push her back into retreat. "Let's go. Let's go. Come on!"

Everyone moved toward the back exit, and that's when the doors blew open in showers of glass and metal.

In came the Protectors on their mission of slaughter.

CHAPTER 15

The two Protectors hit the place like a proper weapons squad conducting a raid on a hostile target. The Protectors let loose, rolling into the store, treads crunching, shooting blue and pink lasers into the place, saturating the entire area with thermogenic beams that crashed and splashed and burned through furniture, scorching walls.

Fires caught as tables and sofas, cabinets, nightstands, and the whole works were crackling and shattering. Laser beams winged and zinged and smoked trails through the place. Explosions detonated, stuffing was ripped apart and sent flying in clouds of flames. Springs sprung from mattresses. The television erupted in a bang of glass and electronic parts.

The air was misty and hot as the Protectors cycled on rapid fire, shooting anything and everything.

Suzie and Greg were in the crosshairs of a ray attack, the lasers slicing around them, landing with sparks and booms that shook the place. Suzie ducked behind a sofa.

"No!" Greg said, knowing full well that sofa was the worst place to seek cover. He was right. As soon as Suzie moved from her hiding spot, the sofa was fried by both pink and blue lasers that split the couch into an inferno of wood chips and leaping fragments.

"Go, go, go, go!" Greg shouted.

Ferdy and Alison vaulted a king-size bed just as a hail of pink and blue whipped apart the mattress in an explosion of flames and sparks. The impact sent them hurtling together to crash into a glass-top coffee table.

Luckily, they hadn't gotten too banged up or scratched; they got to their feet in record time and made quick on their escape. But it seemed they would never reach safety in time. The distance to the stockroom felt like a mile away, a separation made more hazardous by the constant stream of laser beams.

Linda and Rick, hand-in-hand, weaved and ducked and swung aside as countless lasers danced and sang and whistled near, crashing and exploding, blowing holes in the walls.

Alison and Ferdy were on their heels.

Suzie and Greg reached the stockroom doors and were shouting, "Hurry! Hurry up, they're right behind you!"

The Protectors were rolling, their path made clear as lasers blew open a clean passage.

Linda and Rick rushed past Greg, making it to the safety of the back room. Alison and Ferdy were hustling, ducking as incoming lasers sliced the air overhead and shaved closely at their flanks. They made it to the door just in time. Before the mechanical nightmares could reach anyone, Greg slammed the doors shut, just as a barrage of lasers splashed against them.

* * *

Sweating, panting, shaking, everyone was out of their heads with terror. They couldn't understand what was happening. The robots had gone haywire, and they were attacking, but why?

"Poor Leslie," Suzie whimpered. "She didn't deserve that!"

Chopping Mall

Ferdy and Rick were helping Greg pile whatever they could find in front of the doors. They heaped a sizable mattress against it, hoping it would work for the time being.

"Think it'll hold?" Ferdy asked.

Greg ordered more boxes and whatever else they could move to fortify it. Alison, Linda, Rick, Ferdy, and Greg were working to push, shove, and throw whatever was near them against that door. When they were finished, they had constructed quite a mountain of defense. But would it hold?

"Where's Mike?" Suzie asked, quivering in a corner, holding herself.

Everyone regarded each other. Leslie was outside the store, which meant Mike had to have been too. Meaning he probably had met the same fate as Leslie. They all seemed to realize this sad truth at the same time.

"I'm not sure how long this will hold." Greg said, changing the subject. He eyed the barrier, seemingly convinced of its durability. "Those robots have weapons, and it's only a matter of time before they get in here."

"You got any better ideas?" Rick asked him.

Linda was looking around, searching for an exit, clearly putting her mind to work on a solution. "What about a fire exit?"

Greg shook his head, hands on his hips. "All that's gonna do is put us back out in the mall with those machines. We need to think of something else."

Linda sighed. "Well, it beats being trapped in here. Who knows what they're planning out there right now."

Backing his wife, Rick butted in. "Linda's right. We've gotta get out somewhere we can run and get some weapons in our hands. Waiting back here is only asking for trouble."

Everybody froze up. Somewhere, a noise seemed to work its way through the walls and over the ceiling. A vibration of steel cylinders. And, just as suddenly as the vibration started, it was over.

"What was that?" Alison whispered.

Greg said, "That's the sound of us being locked in here all night."

"What do you mean?" Alison asked.

"Those were the security doors to the mall. Has to be. And they don't open back up until six in the morning."

Suzie started to shake violently and sought Greg's arms for comfort. Tears slicked her face, and her lips quivered. "Oh, no. We're never gonna get out of here."

Greg said, "Don't worry, baby, yes we are. We will get out of here."

While everyone was bickering and doing their own thing, Ferdy had the brains to check the phone. He picked it up, listened for a dial tone, then wilted. "Phone's dead. The computer to the security drones must have fried it."

A black silence washed over them. Suzie was still clutching onto Greg.

Alison was checking things out. She didn't search long when she spotted something nobody else saw. "Hey, what about that?"

Greg smiled. "The air duct!"

Ferdy said: "Perfect! We can take it down to the parking level, and we'll be outta here! We just have to get through the gate. But that won't be too hard with all of us."

"Sounds good to me. Let's go for it!" Linda said.

Everybody was in agreement.

They would hop into the air duct, make their way silently through its passages and plop into the parking sectors. It had to be a sure thing. To wait around in the stockroom was asking for it. Those machines wouldn't let them sit around forever, they were bound to blow their way inside, and soon. After the mess they made of Furniture King, it was surprising they hadn't yet crashed the party and smoked them dead.

* * *

The Protectors were smart enough to know the humans had fortified the doors with an abundance of material. But what the humans didn't know was that the Protectors were built, prepared, and equipped for anything.

One of the machines extended its claw, brushing the hinge of the door and squirting out a line of something like hot clay along the length of the hinge. The Protector repeated this with each hinge, then retreated a few feet back, firing wires into each gray smudge.

"PREPARE FOR DETONATION," Protector One said.

Protector Two evacuated the area.

"PROCEEDING TO ALTERNATE ACCESS," said Protector Two.

As Protector Two exited Furniture King to check on an alternate avenue of escape, the Protector One activated the charge, and the doors disappeared in a smoky explosion.

* * *

Alison was struggling to get into the shaft. But, as the explosion blew open the doors, she was hoisted inside quick. She looked behind her and saw the red visor emerging through the haze of the doors. Blue lasers started flashing into the stockroom as mechanical gears cranked and the treads spun.

Greg, Ferdy, and Rick were still in the stockroom, and now they were shit out of luck. They would never make the ventilation shaft in time. They had to think and think fast, and it was Greg who led the charge.

"Come on! Let's get out of here!"

Ferdy saw where Greg was pointing, and he sprinted off, ducking lasers, his hands cupped around behind his head. Rick followed, and Greg went after him, their escape a narrow corridor boxed with supplies. They made it halfway down when Greg's shoulder was sliced open by a laser, blood splashing the wall.

He screamed. But it didn't stop him. A moment later, they were out of sight of the Protector and its deadly aim.

* * *

Alison's hands were starting to burn with each dragging pull through the claustrophobic tunnel. The metal beneath her hands and knees was scorching hot. "I thought this was an air conditioning duct." Another wince and gritting of her teeth. "Why does it feel like the heat has been turned on high?"

"In the middle of summer?" Linda queried, moving in tandem with Alison and feeling the heat against her palms too.

Suzie had it figured out. "They know we're in here. They're trying to French fry us!"

"*Damn!*" Linda said.

"Wrap whatever you can around your hands," Alison told them both, taking her own advice and pulling her sleeves down to her palms.

Suzie didn't have the proper clothing. Sweat greased her face and dropped from her chin, sizzling as it hit the metal plating. "I can't stand this anymore. I gotta get outta here. It's too much."

CHAPTER 16

Paul and Mary—still dressed in the same clothes from the video demonstration—were slowly backing a U-Haul truck into a delivery bay in back of the Mall under cover of night. Paul was driving and could barely see anything in front of him, let alone anything behind him in the mirror of the U-Haul. He was trying to back to the loading dock closest to his restaurant.

Mary was biting her nails again, worrying them to nubs. "Paul, are you sure about this? I mean...are you really sure?"

He kept his eyes on the loading dock, hearing the sound of the storm outside, the wind slapping against the truck, causing it to rock on its springs. "Absolutely, Mary. The meat will be fresh, tasty...and it's much more economical this way. Think about it. Think about the possibilities!"

"But what about the critic from 'Coffee Shop Review'?" Mary said. "He's due in tomorrow morning. What if he detects..."

Paul wasn't worried about some two-bit writer and his opinions stamping the column of some third-rate newspaper no one bothered to read. The only thing Paul cared about was that this was a surefire way to put some extra digits in his checking account. "Stop worrying so much, Mary. What could he possibly say? What damage can he do? We're serving the folks of this mall a decent meal for a decent dollar. Ain't nothing wrong with that. Who cares where the meat comes from?"

Coming to the bumper pads of the loading dock, Paul eased off the brake and felt the connection.

Without a word, both of them went outside in the rain and wind, ducking, coming around the steps. They stood together at the tailgate. Mary jumped as lightning flashed and thunder groaned.

Paul wasn't bothered by any of it. He was already in motion as the rain pecked at his slicker and the lightning flashed overhead. He put his hand on the lever and pulled. It was stuck tight.

"Mary, help me out here."

She did and after several tries, they got it loose. The door swung up on its track, and they stared into a shadow-packed cargo hold. Paul clicked the light switch on.

"Paul, what's the matter with Brewster?" She was searching for the right words. "He seems so...tentative."

Paul shrugged with a laugh, wiping beads of rain off his face. "Gee, I can't imagine why."

Taking Brewster's reins, Paul led the old horse out of the cargo trailer, and walked him to the foot of the service door. "Mary, you mind sliding your key card in the slot so we can get inside?"

Brewster's dark coat was getting washed by the rain, his ears flicking against the wind.

"Sure. I got it," she said.

She used her key, and then they were inside a service corridor where it was dry and warm. They could hear the storm outside banging against the door, the pebbling spray of rain. Paul led Brewster along, as Mary trailed behind the horse's rear-end. They had gone half-way down the hall when Brewster's tail arched, and out plopped a steaming mound the size of a bundt cake.

"Oh, Brewster, couldn't you have done that outside?" Mary said.

Paul laughed it off. "Now, Mary, I think he's behaving remarkably well considering the circumstances."

"But, Paul, I—"

"Shush, Mary, there's no need to alert those little mechanical ruffians to our activities. Mall personnel would certainly frown on it, don't you think? Besides, Brewster here doesn't have a security badge, and I'm not sure how the Protectors would respond to that. That Simon fellow wasn't clear about animals."

Coming to the end of the service corridor, Paul slowed the pace and pressed the door, opening it slightly and peering out. A quick look left and right was all he needed to feel positive they were alone.

"See anything?" Mary whispered just below him, poking her head out of the door so that his chin nearly rested on her head.

Paul didn't, but he still wanted to be careful before advancing any further. "Nothing obvious, but you just don't know. They're crafty from what I've heard."

"Let's keep looking for a little bit, they're devious little bastards, I just know it."

Brewster whinnied.

Paul turned his head a little, whispering: "Brewster! Will you please keep quiet back there? You'll tip our hand!"

Mary added, "Listen to Paul, Brewster. He knows what's best for you."

Suddenly, something slammed into Brewster from behind like sixty pounds of dynamite. It ripped through him, literally blowing him open in an explosion of smoking meat and hot blood, intestines on fire, flying and sticking to the wall. Paul and Mary were violently blown back from the door. Paul hit the neighboring wall with terminal velocity, his head bashed into a smear.

Mary's back took a blast of bone shards the size of steak knives, and they ripped her arms and legs away, opened her backside, and smashed her spine to soup.

Brewster, Mary, and Paul all died instantly.

Smoke settled in a service corridor thick with blood, hair, smoke, and meat, and little tufts of crushed velvet. The only thing left standing were four horse legs cut away at the knees.

"LOWER-LEVEL SERVICE CORRIDOR, CLEARED OF INTRUDERS. HAVE A NICE DAY."

CHAPTER 17

Reaching the end of the stockroom's exit, Greg yanked the door open, and they all hurried out in a disorienting jumble of strained breathing and rapid heartbeats. Somewhere during the escape, Rick had armed himself with a crowbar, and he held it in both hands, ready to swing on anything made of bolts and metal.

Rick, prepared to crack machines to sparks, switched his eyes left and right, surveying his surroundings, his head cocking at every sound, his voice laced with fear. "What now?"

Greg checked on the wound to his shoulder. The laser must have cauterized it because there was no blood, just a painful scabbing rough as sandpaper. "First thing's first, we find the girls and then look for a way out of here."

"Ain't gonna be so easy without a way to defend ourselves." Rick countered. "Does this place have any sporting goods stores?"

Greg and Ferdy shared a look, a gleam of hope in their eyes. Together, they said: "Peckinpah's!"

***

The path to Peckinpah's was far too long for anyone's comfort. All three of their heads were on a constant swivel. They maneuvered in the shadows of planters and stuck close to the store fronts. Several times they took a knee or crouched out of sight when they heard the mechanical whirring sounds.

Ferdy, Rick, and Greg moved along like hunted things, their hearts in their throats, the thought of their women at the forefront of their worries.

The three swung around a corner, and up ahead was their target; Peckinpah's Sporting Goods. They came to a stop, looking to their flanks, making sure they were in the clear before they made themselves completely visible.

Rick raised his crowbar up. "Don't worry, I got the keys."

He ran forward and smashed the glass door open.

Ferdy put his hands up to guard his face. "Jesus."

Not a second was wasted standing there. They moved inside, scurrying, looking for anything worthy of putting up a fight against the killer robots.

Greg fired off orders to Ferdy. "Grab some propane tanks if you can find them. Make sure you get the biggest there is."

"All right."

Rick spotted the firearms, and his eyes jacked open. Peckinpah's had everything he could have hoped for. Shotguns, automatic rifles, pistols—thank the Lord for 1980s America, he thought.

His hands immediately went to the Mossberg 12 bore. He looked it over, seeing boxes of shells within reach. It would be a perfect weapon, something that packed a serious punch. He just needed the right shells.

Greg was there too, his eyes landing squarely on the rack of automatic rifles. Taking an M-16, he held it the same way a soldier would have, bringing the stock into his shoulder, one hand on the grip, finger hooking the trigger, the other hand cupped under the hand-guard. He laid his eye down the sights, getting a feel for its accuracy. This would do well. With its range, he'd be able to tag those things where it counted. Taking handfuls of magazines, he started thumbing in cartridges.

On his own, Ferdy scored some propane tanks, grabbing what he could and leaving behind plenty. Heading up front, he stopped at a shelving unit displaying various handguns. One in particular caught his eye. Setting the tanks down, he took the weapon, an eight-inch Smith .357 nickel. He had seen this exact revolver in many action movies, including his favorite: *Dirty Harry*.

Lower on the shelving unit were boxes upon boxes of ammunition. He scooped up several, loading the cylinder, and pocketing the rest. Now, he was ready for anything.

Several minutes passed in a blur as the three of them regrouped and prepared for the coming battle. They were like kids living out some morbid fantasy, stockpiling for an invasion of evil. They were the last vanguard, a race of warriors engaged in the final war against the machines. They would fight, rescue their women, and be celebrated as heroes of the Park Plaza Mall.

Together, they had bandoleers, bullets, magazines, and enough propane to level a good portion of the mall.

Armed and confident, the trio left the shattered entry of Peckinpah's and stood together, shoulder-to-shoulder, a contingent of fighters ready to confront the menace of the machine invaders.

Rick was the first one to break their silence. "Let's go send those fuckers a Rambo-gram."

They ran off, neon shading overlapping their advance. Every step along the way, they felt fingers of tension at their backs and working into their hearts. They might have been armed, ready for battle, but even the fantasy hadn't fully empowered them. There was still the very real possibility they might fail, or the weapons wouldn't leave a scratch. But they had to deep-six those feelings, erase them before they got the better of their emotions.

They came to a stop in an open court. Looking around, weapons ready, Greg saw the magnum in Ferdy's hands and asked him: "You sure you know how to shoot that thing?"

Grinning a yard wide, Ferdy spun the revolver in his hand. "Yeah. Of course I know how to shoot it. I've seen *Dirty Harry* twenty-four times."

That didn't prove anything, but Greg wasn't about to shatter the confidence. They needed every bit of it they could get.

"All set?" Rick asked them, shotgun poised in his hands.

Greg ran a quick visual over his M-16, slapping it. "I'm good."

Ferdy nodded, the magnum thrust ahead as if he were sighting in on a horde of rushing bad guys. "Ready as rain."

Rick nodded. "Good." He jerked the trigger on the shotgun, pumped it, and blew off a slug.

Their ears ringing, Greg smiled uneasily. "They had to have heard that."

"Dead men could have heard *that*," Ferdy added.

They didn't have to wait long. Barely a minute passed when one of the Protectors arrived on the scene, wheeling its way in direct line of them, the red visor vibrant against the shadowed backdrop.

Ferdy saw it and said as much. "Hey, fellas, we got company."

"Little fucker showed up faster than I thought it would," Greg said, setting the rifle's stock firmly into his shoulder.

While holding their ground, spread abreast, Rick said, "Steady now. Wait for it to get closer." They all watched, their fingers hooking the triggers. "Go for it!"

Boom! Pop! Bam!

Bullets contested with pink laser beams. Lead bounced off

the surface of the machine. Some of the shots made headway, denting or drilling into the carapace, winging off the plating. But overall, they didn't do much.

Pink fire blazed at them. Greg leaped behind some wall cover, swinging his shotgun around and cranking off rounds.

Ferdy and Rick found a stout pillar of concrete, their guns cracking as smoke and flames and sparks pulled together to create a hazy wall in front of them. The red visor was all they could see. Pink lasers roamed into the haze, firing wildly, blowing store windows to dust, setting displays on fire, scorching walls.

"What do we do?" Ferdy shouted over a blast of his revolver.

Rick pointed to one of the tanks. "Roll that thing over to it!"

Of course, the propane tanks. Ferdy shoved the magnum in his belt and took one big white tank in both hands. In a motion like he was bowling with two hands, he rolled it over, and it clanged against the Protector's treads.

Rick popped out of his hiding spot, racked and pumped the shotgun, and sent a volley of slugs. One of them hit its mark and pierced the tank. The tank exploded into a wall of flame and smoke that engulfed the machine. All at once, the lasers stopped, and everything was suddenly quiet.

CHAPTER 18

Suzie couldn't stop with her constant whining. There was no end to it. She would cry out, say something about Greg and the heat of the ventilation shaft, then start all over again. She was cracking, and Linda and Alison were having a hard time keeping her together.

"I gotta find Greg," she said for the fifth time. "He needs me."

Alison snapped. "Suzie, please! The guys told us to go down to the parking levels, remember? That's probably where they're at."

"Come on, kiddo," Linda said, trying to encourage Suzie. "Greg wouldn't want you to give up now. You have to keep going."

"Oh, go to hell, Linda! You do what you want, but I'm getting out of here. None of you are going to stop me!"

"Suzie, stop it! Please!" Alison shouted, her own voice starting to crack.

Suzie stopped when she noticed a mesh screen below her. It led to one of the stores in the mall. She wasn't sure which one, but it didn't matter at this point. Another minute in that shaft, and she would be done, broken open completely.

She punched the screen four times before it gave and fell into the store. "Greg needs me. I know he does!"

Alison and Linda watched helplessly as Suzie dropped into the store.

* * *

A stack of smoke billowed off the dead Protector, its visor shut down, its body knocked to the side. Greg and Ferdy joined Rick who had already made the distance over to the machine, his eyes all steel satisfaction.

The smell of gunpowder in the air was spliced with burnt circuitry.

They all stood around the Protector as snakes of blue electricity swam around its shell. Greg opened another round on it, striking it with two shots. Ferdy fell in line, and his magnum BOOMED and punched a hole through it. Rick slammed it with a slug, and it was good as dead. At least they hoped it was.

"Jesus," Rick said, shaking his head.

"What's that?" Ferdy pointed to a spreading black pool pouring from the machine's bottom side.

"Robot blood," Greg said.

"Not too shabby, huh?" Ferdy said, feeling the power back in his hands.

"Yeah. Well, we're not finished yet," Greg said. There were still two more of these evil robots rolling about the mall. "Remember, this wasn't the only one. It's got friends, and we need to find them."

"I think we're going to need more tanks," Rick said.

"What are you thinking?" Ferdy asked him.

His eyes brightened. He looked at his friends; a scheme was clearly brewing. "I got an idea."

***

The relief they felt was instant the moment they left the ventilation shaft. It had to be true that the robots somehow sabotaged the system because every minute the duct was getting hotter.

The girls found themselves in a store of paint cans, power tools, construction supplies; they were in the mall's hardware store, The Paint and the Pendulum.

There was no telling where those machines could be. They were sneaky things, and it wouldn't surprise any of the girls if the Protectors had set up an ambush in there for them.

Alison was jumpy. There were too many shadows, too many hiding places. "Really, you guys, this is not a good idea."

"*Bullshit!*" Suzie screamed, no longer caring about anything but reuniting with her boyfriend. They came out of an aisle. "Greg could be hurt. They all could be in terrible danger. I'm gonna find them. I've got to!"

Linda paused to get her bearings. She hadn't stopped to think about where they'd landed. "You know," she said. "A hardware store could provide many things that could give us an edge. If we gotta go find the boys..." she started picking through material on the shelves. "Let's not go empty-handed."

CHAPTER 19

Back in Peckinpah's, the three guys restocked their ammo, grabbed whatever else they could carry with them, and were soon back out in the mall. Greg and Ferdy were struggling to keep up with Rick who was bolting to the nearest elevator.

Finally, they reached the elevator nearly out of breath. Greg tried the button to the door.

"Shit, it's not working."

The guys were stumped, but there had to be a way. Full functionality to the mall's conveyance system wasn't centralized to one computer. There were emergency backups running on their own boards. And much more primitive methods to gain entry.

Ferdy said, "Never hurts to try," then he slid his fingers into the groove between the elevator doors, and started straining.

"No, I guess not," Greg said.

"Give me a hand, guys," Ferdy said. "Let's pry this baby open."

Together, they put their muscles into it, prying, pulling, teeth grinding, giving it everything they had and then some.

"Come on!" Greg shouted at the door.

"You know, I got a bit of a worry," Ferdy said, fingers deeper in the gap now.

"Report from the front—Ferdy's got a worry," Greg said sarcastically.

"Yeah?" Rick said.

"Look, you guys, what if these things can read our minds? I've seen in it a movie once."

Rick eyed Ferdy seriously. "If they could see into mine, they'd die from fright."

That's when doors finally gave way, bucked from their casing, and slid back smoothly.

"All right!" said Greg.

"Come on. Let's go!" said Rick.

They piled in. Now was the time to set things in motion.

* * *

While her husband was tinkering with the ultimate elevator trap, Linda was taking care of things in The Paint and the Pendulum. She was in boss mode, directing Alison and Suzie.

"Take the cap off, and stuff the cloth inside, see?" Linda instructed them how to make Molotov cocktails with a simple show-and-tell presentation as if she were teaching a class about the subtle components of radical arson.

"That's it?" Alison said.

"That's it," Linda told her with a smile. "Just light it, throw it —BOOM!"

Suzie looked up to Linda. "Sounds like you've done this thing before."

"Regular or unleaded," Linda said. "It gets the job done."

"I'm not sure I'm doing this right," Suzie stammered.

"It's okay, Suzie, you're doing just fine."

Suzie looked away, wiping tears. "Thanks."

Chopping Mall

Alison tightened the cap on her Molotov. She stretched and looked away from her work, and that's when she caught sight of a display shelf. Flares, dozens of them, sat in neat rows in an open box. She took a walk and grabbed one, checking it over. She ran her finger over the thick plastic topper, then surreptitiously slipped a flare into her bra.

* * *

Smoke continued to gush from the shell of Protector One. Sparks still flecked from the gash on its underside. But it wasn't out of the fight just yet. The robot began rocking and the gears began turning. Soon Protector One was back on its tread. Its visor, though cracked, was still functional, meaning its laser cannon was ready to kill. Its head swiveled as if working out the kinks. Its system rebooted.

"PROTECTOR ONE BACK ONLINE."

* * *

Crouching on the top of the elevator, Greg and Rick busied themselves stringing propane tanks together. Rick told Greg and Ferdy this contraption would work perfectly. He explained they would lure the robot into the elevator and detonate the tanks, and BOOM, the whole thing, including any Protectors would go up in a fireball of molten metal.

Ferdy was down below them, busy rigging the control panel, rewiring it so the robot couldn't counter their trap by opening the door back up once it was inside.

"Hey, guys, how's it goin'?" Ferdy asked.

"Almost done, Ferdy," Greg shouted. Threading a hose to the nozzle-end of a tank, he turned to Rick. "You think Mike got out okay?"

"For his sake, I hope so," Rick said. "But right now, I'm more concerned about the girls."

"Yeah, you and me both. Hey, I almost forgot. How much do I owe you for the beer you brought?"

Rick smiled, or at least tried to under the circumstances. "Heh. Forget it, man. We get out of here, you owe *me* a six-pack —just make sure those cords are good and tight on those tanks."

"Yeah. You're certain this is gonna work?"

"With those crazy fuckin' robots, I'm not sure of anything. But it has to do something."

"Hey, Ferdy, how's the panel job coming along?" Greg asked.

"Well, the doors are working just fine now. I bypassed the circuit easy enough. But forget about going up or down."

"Do you hear anything unusual down there?" Greg asked.

"Only my heartbeat," Ferdy said.

CHAPTER 20

The girls tried to sneak out the back of The Paint and the Pendulum, but the second they emerged, a Protector appeared, as if it had been waiting for them the entire time. It blew the door off with its laser. Suzie screamed, ran. Linda and Alison followed closely behind her. The metal monster gave chase. Its visor shot out lasers as it hunted them.

The girls wasted no time in going to work, lugging bombs while screaming. They exited the winding halls of the employee area and found their way back into the main area of the mall again. They were making good speed, but the Protector was gaining and gaining, slinging laser beams, shooting up the surrounding stores, ripping windows to smoking mist.

Burdened by the weight of their equipment, they were slower than normal, so Linda brought them to a halt and shared her thoughts. They needed to make a stand—because running *clearly* wasn't working. This was a time of reckoning; to prove they could defeat this machine.

Seeking cover, Suzie and Alison scurried behind a barrier of planters and cement pillars as Linda sidled up behind a single pillar screaming for Alison to toss a bomb.

Doing as she was told, Alison flicked the lighter and put the flame on the rag. Once it caught, she hurled it like a football, and it detonated with an explosive wave of flames. The Protector came to a sudden halt, and the girls breathed a collective sigh of relief. It was short-lived however, because the Protector shot through the smoky screen and started blasting every which way it could.

Suzie screamed, "It's not stopping!"

Linda hurled another bomb, and it ignited and spread flames over the Protector's body. But nothing else happened.

Neon blue lasers zapped and screeched and banged against metal and cement and glass, streaking across the carpeting, causing fires to rip open the flooring.

The girls exchanged glances, left their cover and made a run for it. Suzie took a laser to the calf.

She screamed and hit the ground, landing on her face, and busting open her nose. Blood went down her mouth and chin.

Linda and Alison leaped to cover, turned back and saw Suzie flat on the floor, her face bloody, her eyes wrenched wide in terror. They attempted to go back for her, but were beaten back by the onslaught of lasers slicing through the air.

"Help me! Somebody help me!"

"Suzie!" Linda screamed, reaching out a hand, knowing damn well it was too dangerous to get to Suzie.

Alison hid and put her hands over her ears. She couldn't listen to this anymore.

"Alison, help! Linda!"

"We've gotta help her!" Linda shouted, blue lasers streaking past, blowing out chunks of stores and flooring.

"THANK YOU, AND HAVE A NICE DAY."

The Protector zeroed in on Suzy and shattered the remaining Molotov cocktail in her hand. The little container exploded, splashing its payload over Suzie who was completely engulfed in flames. Her skin ignited, blackening and sizzling as it became like heated butter, sliding and spattering the ground. With her dying breath, she reached out for help, her finger bones on fire, black smoke rising and twisting overhead.

Linda watched helplessly as Suzie burned alive, crawling to Linda and Alison, leaving behind a trail of slime and embers.

Finally, she stopped, one arm still outstretched, her jaw sprung, eye sockets belching jets of flame.

Alison paled and nearly fainted. She turned away to block out the image, and that's when she saw Ferdy, Rick, and Greg coming toward her with guns blazing. Bullets struck and pinged off the hard casing of the killer machine.

Greg took the lead, shouting at them all to start running away. And right away, he saw Suzie. What was left of her, smeared and burning and popping in the carpet. He lifted his rifle and emptied the magazine in rapid fire.

"YOU FUCKING BASTARD!" he screamed at the machine.

Rick saw what was happening and ordered Ferdy to get the girls back. "Ferdy, get them to safety! Go! We'll be right behind you!"

As Ferdy fell in line, pulling Alison and Linda back out of harm's way, Rick and Greg blasted and blasted, peppering the monster of metal with everything they had. But in the end, no matter how many bullets or perfect shots they fired, it wasn't doing a damn thing. The Protector countered and opened up with automatic laser cannons, showering the way ahead with a spray of blue death.

"Forget it, man! It's no use!" Rick said, taking Greg by the shoulder and forcing him to retreat.

Before he pulled away, Greg saw the thing roll over the pile of his girlfriend. Then he turned and ran. In their mad dash, they made it to the elevator just as Ferdy, Alison, and Linda took cover a short distance away.

Rick ordered Greg to toss him the M-16. Greg sent the weapon in an arc that landed right in Rick's hands. In return, Rick had tossed his shotgun to Greg.

Breaking away, Greg raced over to the others, getting behind cover.

Rick went into the elevator just as the Protector came around the corner, its visor still blasting blue lasers in all directions.

Rick ran into the elevator and sealed the doors behind him. Then he threw the M-16 through the gap in the ceiling and pulled himself up and out so he was on top of the elevator.

Just as Rick made it through the ceiling shaft, the Protector pried the doors open, and rolled inside, clearly confused by the empty room. Before it could escape, the doors closed, sealing it in.

Feeling in control, Rick steadied himself and jumped from the roof, clearing ten feet of open space, and landed on the floor with a roll. He came up and shouted to the others. "Guys, open fire on the tanks!"

They did. Greg and Linda and Ferdy blasted away, with Rick jerking the trigger on the M-16. Their accuracy was for shit.

Alison made a move, taking Ferdy's magnum as he fired off a shot—

"Hey!" Ferdy said.

She ignored him, lined her sights, exhaled, and dropped the hammer. The heavy slug struck the tank, and a roaring detonation sent a forty-foot fireball up in the air, and dropped an ocean of flames and metal into the elevator itself.

The elevator cables snapped, and its car went screaming down to the lower levels. When it hit the bottom, another explosion and a huge pillar of smoke and sparks and flames belched out of the shaft.

Chopping Mall

Everything was quiet after that.
Ferdy was looking at Alison with love. "Nice shot."
Alison blew on the muzzle. "Dad was a Marine."

CHAPTER 21

Greg busted the lock of La Signora In Rosso with a blast of his shotgun. They all went inside, left the lights off, and sat around after pushing some tables against the windows and doors.

"That leaves only one of those bastards," Ferdy said. "We're gonna make it, you guys."

"Even if we do, according to my calculations," Linda said. "We're gonna be in debt to this place for the next eighty-five years."

Rick jacked in a fresh magazine in the M-16. "Hey, dead-eye," Rick called to Alison.

"Yo," she said, her eyes filmy, tired, spent.

"Nice shooting."

She forced a smile. "Thanks."

"Fuck that," Greg's voice was angry. All eyes were suddenly on him. "Tell me one thing, *Dead-Eye*." His tone was dripping with sarcasm. "Why did you leave the air vents? You were safe inside there, right? You were *SAFE!*"

"Greg," Alison started. "The vents were hot as hell. We had to leave. And Suzie was sure you were in trouble. She just wanted to help you—"

Greg raged. "I'm telling you that you should've kept her in there! It was stupid of you to let her leave!"

Ferdy leaned forward. "Look, she told you what happened, Greg. Why don't you just leave her alone? She has nothing to do with—"

"*Shut up*," Greg said flat and cold as the grave. "You just shut the *fuck* up!"

"Hey," Rick whisper-shouted, standing up. He got in between the three of them quickly. "Do you mind keeping it down? There's another one of those things out there—" he looked over to Greg for emphasis "—and *you're* gonna bring it right to us if you keep this up."

Linda's eyes went wide. "There's another one?"

"Why haven't we seen it?" Alison asked.

"Why?" Greg said, his voice cracking. "I'll tell you *why*. 'Cause the fucker's out there waiting for us, that's why! He's waiting to pick us off one by one!" Greg pulled a shell from his pocket. "But I got news for you." He held the shell up to his eye before slotting it in the chamber. "He ain't getting *me*. Oh no, he ain't getting me."

"Greg, you're not thinking, man," Rick said. "We got this far by staying together. If we split now, we're done for."

Greg put his palm out to silence any speeches Rick may have had ready. "And a lot of good that did, Suzie, right?" He shot a glance to Alison and Linda. "Sticking together?"

Nobody had anything to add.

"Wait. I got an idea," Ferdy said. "The master computer is somewhere on the third level, right? We shut it down, it shuts the robots down. It has to work!"

"It's worth a try," Rick said.

"Computer mainframe, huh?" Greg thought it over. He jacked the shell into the chamber. "Let's go trash the fucker!"

CHAPTER 22

The plan wasn't foolproof, but it was better than sitting around and waiting for another futile firefight with the robots to come to them. They left the restaurant in a hurry.

"Come on, guys!" Greg shouted, spearheading the group. "Let's shake it!"

Rick, Ferdy, Linda, and Alison could hardly keep up with him. Some spark had sent him flying, and he was too far ahead. Maybe it was the death of Suzie and the prospect of revenge that fired him up.

"Hey, buddy," Rick said, winded by the run. "Slow down!"

Linda said, "Greg, will you wait?!"

"God, man," Ferdy said, trying to catch his breath. "He's losin' it!"

Alison agreed. "We'll be lucky if he doesn't get us all killed!"

Greg came to an escalator and bounded up the steps.

"Greg, stop! Don't go up that way!" Linda shouted.

Ferdy, Rick, Alison, and Linda all came to a stop at the bottom of the escalator.

Greg reached the top and turned, his eyes wild and wet, his

90

Chopping Mall

mouth hooked in an insane grin. "Come on, guys! The coast is clear!"

Alison screamed suddenly. "Greg, watch out!"

A claw clamped down on Greg's bicep, squeezing so hard it cracked the bone and split his skin open. Blood sprayed.

"No!" he screamed, managing to shuck a shell at the machine before it swung him over the railing and released its grip, sending him plunging three stories down.

There was a sickening crack, and Greg's head blew open, blood and brains spraying out all over the first floor.

"THANK YOU. HAVE A NICE DAY."

Rick and Ferdy blew off some rounds.

Alison saw movement below and saw another Protector coming up the escalator. "Oh my God, you guys. There!" she cried. "I thought there was only one left!"

They all saw it coming up the steps.

"Damnit!" Ferdy said. "I thought we killed that one!"

"PROTECTOR ONE TO LEVEL TWO. DETAIN INTRUDERS."

"PROTECTOR THREE TO LEVEL TWO. DETAIN INTRUDERS."

Rick led the way. "Over here!" he said.

He led them to the solid security gate of a department store named Operation Vogue. He lifted the M-16 and capped off six shots that disintegrated the gate's lock. Ferdy grabbed the bottom of the gate and pulled.

"It's stuck!"

Rick laid aside the rifle and helped. "Let's get it unstuck, *fast!*"

"Come on!" Linda said, lending a hand.

"There's no time," Alison insisted. "We're not going to make it!" Over her shoulder, she saw the two Protectors rolling toward them, red visors charged brightly, tiny headlights streaming out from their convex bodies.

Just in time, the gate rolled up its track wide enough to

squeeze through at a ground crawl. Linda rolled through first, followed by Rick. Ferdy went down to his belly, wriggled through, then turned to help Alison through. He pulled her through just as she took a laser beam to her right shoulder.

"Alison!" he screamed.

Green and pink lasers intersected, blasting holes in the gate, sending sparks flying and flaring, glass crashing.

Ferdy and Alison ran into the store.

"Are you okay?" Ferdy asked.

"I think so," she said, but the pain was there in her voice.

"Where to?" Rick asked, taking in their surroundings which was cluttered with clothing racks, jewelry islands, and mannequins posing about.

"Escalator, third level—" Ferdy said.

"What about the doors?" Alison said, her arm dripping blood. "We can't lock them. They'll get through!"

Rick handed his rifle to Linda. "Maybe so." He pried a foot-long metal bar from a display rack and shoved it into the chain sprocket on the gate. "Maybe not."

They all ran off toward the escalator.

* * *

The Protectors, blocked by the gate in front of Operation Vogue began breaching protocols, communicating with the mainframe.

"*INSTRUCTIONS—ATTEMPT ENTRY, LEVEL THREE. AFFIRMATIVE.*"

A latent source in the robot was activated, and a solid pink beam hit the metal door, burning right through it. In a slow arc, the beam cut its way up, slicing through the steel as easily as butter.

As Protector One cut through the security gate, Protector Three headed for the upper level.

* * *

"It's in! It's in the store!" Linda snapped.

"Yeah, and it won't be long before it comes our way," Alison said.

"We've gotta get out of here." Ferdy said.

"Not so fast!" Rick shouted. "One of them could've doubled back. We could get picked off out there. We're going to have to be very careful."

"Well, look," Alison said. "If those things want some target practice, why don't we give 'em some targets?"

CHAPTER 23

Once that door rolled open, Protector Three was ready. Sentinel, immobile, its gears revved. It immediately picked up several life-forms directly in front of it.

But what it failed to register was these targets weren't real lifeforms. Rather, they were mannequins.

The Protector's laser cannon cycled out green bolts in rapid fashion. The mannequins were smelted down to many plastic pools. That's when Rick and Ferdy opened fire on the Protector.

Ferdy yelled over his shoulder to the girls. "Get out of here! Go!"

"Now, Ferdy!" Rick shouted over the sharp reports of his rifle.

They both went into motion, each taking a corner of a bedsheet and yanking it from its position, exposing several square mirrors. A single laser splashed against one, and it deflected, winging back at the Protector.

Immediately, the Protector was engulfed in electric-blue snakes crackling over its frame. The Protector spun on its treads and malfunctioned, shooting lasers in a death blossom.

Linda and Alison beat feet through the store, coming around

Chopping Mall

the flank and making the exit. As Alison kept running, Linda stopped abruptly, turning to see Rick still cranking off shots at the malfunctioning Protector unit.

Alison and Ferdy made it to a safe corner of the store and watched from their vantage point.

Linda watched as the rogue lasers narrowly avoided Rick.

"Watch out!" She screamed. The precise moment the words exited her mouth, she took a laser bolt to the belly, and it blew out her entire midsection in one greasy, red spray. She collapsed, folded right over, so much crimson mist rising out of her stomach.

"LINDA!" Rick screamed. He turned and aimed his M-16 back toward the glitching Protector. "You sonofabitch!" Firing his rifle in one hand, he eyed a security cart nearby. Dodging the lasers, he hopped on the cart, and aimed it right for the Protector, in an attempt to mow the bastard down.

"Rick, no!" Alison screamed.

He wasn't listening. He crashed into the Protector. There was an explosion of blue fire and sparks. Rick tumbled out of the seat of the cart, electricity coursing through his veins. Untold volts ravaged his body, as he convulsed and foamed at the mouth on the floor next to the malfunctioning Protector.

Whatever Rick had done seemed to work. The robot seized up, crackling, sparks bursting, and smoke rolling from a dozen places.

Rick and Linda were dead. Their mutilated, sizzling bodies were still smoking.

Ferdy and Alison turned their eyes from the sight. They needed to keep moving. They needed to reach their objective.

Ferdy took her by the hand. "Let's go find that computer."

CHAPTER 24

"Where the hell is this place?" Alison asked, panting.

"Probably off one of these service corridors," Ferdy said.

Of course, it didn't help that there were several corridors, and they were running out of time before the last Protector eventually showed up.

"There's a million doors, Ferdy! We'll never find it! What if I try over there? And you try over here."

Ferdy's eyes widened. "No, we can't split up. It's too dangerous."

"What's the worst that can happen?"

"You want a list?"

"We're wasting time," she told him. "We can't just stand here and bicker. We need to make more progress."

Ferdy finally relented. "Okay, look, if you even think you see anything or hear anything bad, you just—"

"You'll hear me," she said, putting a finger to his lips.

* * *

Chopping Mall

The service corridor was a passage of shadows and dim lighting. It snaked one way and another, leading off behind all the stores and opening into stockrooms and loading bays.

Alison could feel the dread pressing against her. All alone, a scared little girl in a big bad haunted house, she moved ahead, staying close to the wall.

She halted when she heard a banging sound, like metal clanging on metal. Her eyes jumped from down the corridor to a side door on her left where this sound was coming from. Should she investigate it or let it be? Maybe it was Mike?

A security cart was nearby, and she plucked a steel pipe from its tray, then approached the door. She twisted and yanked it open. She leaped back in time as a heap of cleaning supplies and tube lights came spilling out on the ground in a loose pile.

She heard a noise behind her. She spun, and screamed. It was a Protector! The Protector raised its arms, its visor painted the area red.

Alison screamed. "FERDY! HELP FERDY!"

CHAPTER 25

The smallness of the area had closed around her tight as a fist. The Protector had cut her off. There would be no escape this time. No angle to use. Nothing. She was hamstrung, screaming, the pipe in her hand shaking. She dropped it as the Protector came closer, its arms up, pincers slicing the air, visor superheated red.

She wondered why the machine hadn't killed her yet.

"Ferdy, help!"

Then he did. He seemed to come out of nowhere, storming right through the door, eyes up, magnum in hand. He kicked the Protector from behind, and the killer robot spun around to meet him. Ferdy didn't even blink. He fired a slug right into its visor, point blank, shattering it like glass. The Protector's body spun and spun in a circle, arms wigging out.

"Alison, move, get out of there!"

"LASER MALFUNCTION. DETAIN INTRUDERS."

Alison waited for an opening and bolted past the machine. But her timing was off. She screamed as its arms hit her, the claws cutting her back and shoulder open.

"DETAIN INTRUDER. LASER MALFUNCTION. LASER MALFUNCTION."

With Alison at his back now, Ferdy shot off two more slugs that punched into the robot's visor, blowing it out in a red flash of light.

"*Detain intruder. Detain intruder.*"

Together, Ferdy and Alison rushed down the service corridor, hearts in their throats, the sound of the machine just behind them, bumping into the wall as it tried to orient itself.

"*Stop right there.*"

Ferdy and Alison blasted out of the door that had led to the service corridor. They were back in the main part of the mall again, and it wasn't long before the Protector joined them. The goddamn thing just wouldn't stop. Ferdy faced the mechanical menace once more and fired his last shots, then tossed the gun in a final act of defiance.

Alison watched in nervous terror as Ferdy prepared to fight against the machine with no weapon. "*Ferdy!*"

"Alison, get the hell out of here!" he shouted as he ran to a nearby wall and pulled a fire extinguisher from its emergency case. Alison did as she was told. She ran off, finding cover.

Ferdy flung the fire extinguisher at the robot. Its claw caught the object in mid-air and pitched it back where it hit Ferdy like a rocket, knocking him off his feet and sending him wheeling through the air. He hit the ground, face down, with a sickening thud.

He stopped moving, and Alison muffled a scream.

The Protector rolled over to his body and stopped to assess. From her hiding spot, Alison could see a heavy amount of blood spreading beneath Ferdy's face.

She wanted to crawl into a hole and die.

"*Thank you. Have a nice day.*"

CHAPTER 26

Alone now.

All by herself, pursued by a death machine. The mall was silent, a graveyard of shadows and horror. Just her and the killer robot now.

There was nowhere to hide, nowhere to go.

But she had to find a place just to think, to collect her thoughts and figure out her next move if she wanted to survive. As she ran through the mall, trying to stick to the shadows, she saw Roger's Little Shop of Pets on her right. A pet store? It was better than nothing. Maybe the movement and sounds from the animals would camouflage her presence there.

But how to get inside? Then she saw the key: a standing ashtray. One of those *glorious* cylindrical three-foot-tall containers that were spread throughout the mall. She picked it up and ran over to the doors. She tossed it at the door, the glass cascaded down like a waterfall. And then she was inside, moving past rows of pet supplies, rabbits, birds, snakes, barking puppies, purring kitties, and fish tanks with colorful fishes.

She ran to the reptile display in the back. She looked around, looking for a place to hide. Then she saw it; a horizontal gap in the shelving. It was around two-feet high and eight-feet long, and plugged up with heavy bags of feed and various supplies. She pulled these out and crawled in, dragging it all back against her, so that it boxed her in. She hoped the machine couldn't find her.

Then she heard it. Even above the animals in the store going nuts at her invasion, she heard the mechanical noises. She heard its treads crunching glass shards as it entered the store. And crazy enough, the animals stopped squawking, as if even *they* were scared.

She could hear it getting close. It began tearing the place apart with its metal claws, trying to find her. As it rolled deeper into the store, it demolished the cashier stations, knocked over a merch stand, and smashed the glass on the animal enclosures.

Alison saw the Protector out of the corner of her eye, rolling slowly into the reptile zone. It sat there, silently for a moment.

That's when Alison realized she wasn't alone with the robot now, because its assault had freed the spiders and snakes which now found solace in the heat of her skin, crawling up her legs and arms. She had to bite her tongue not to scream. But it was the hardest thing in the world to do right then.

She was on the edge. *Over* the edge, actually, and only barely hanging on by a pinky finger.

And then, miracle of miracles, the Protector seemed to lose interest and began backing out of the area. She waited, listening to its treads spin, as the sound faded until it was completely out of the store.

It took her more than a few minutes to emerge from her cover. Even as spiders scurried over her. Eventually, she crawled out from her hiding place, batting away bugs and snakes and spiders the size of hockey pucks.

On her feet, she moved through the store carefully, cautiously, alert to every sound. Things rolled off destroyed shelves. Birds were squawking, feathers floating in the air. There were the charred remains of animals she couldn't make out.

Smoke hung in the air, and it was difficult to see even a few feet ahead. Shelving stations were knocked over, the whole store looked like an explosion had ripped it apart. She stepped out of the pet store, and immediately realized she'd made a mistake. The Protector had been waiting, and it gave chase.

Alison screamed and ran.

Up ahead, she came to an opening. It was the top floor food court. And the only way out was down. Alison grabbed the railing and swung herself over the side. Then she slowly lowered herself until her body was no longer visible, and her feet were hanging over an abyss of space. She held on for dear life, hoping not to be found.

She heard the Protector come into the area, roving around, searching for her. It was knocking over tables, crashing into things. When it sounded like there was some safe distance between her and the machine, she pulled herself slightly up and looked.

She saw the Protector was much closer than she'd anticipated. It swung its head towards her, and she almost lost her hold, lowering again immediately so she wouldn't be discovered. Her muscles strained, sweat beaded on her face, her fingers were white as bone, and her teeth were gritting.

Unsure of how much longer she could hold on, she looked below, and noticed she was lined up with a white and blue tarp that had been erected. She hoped it would cushion her fall because she had completely run out of strength.

She lost her grip and fell two floors, smacking into the tarp, which thankfully, was soft, and somewhat helped cushion her fall. The thing collapsed around her, blanketing over her. She came out of the middle with the wind knocked out of her. She got right to her feet, sharp pains pulsing all over her body.

Suddenly, she remembered the signal flare she'd stuck in her bra. She checked it to make sure it was there.

It was! She couldn't believe it. And just like that, she had a plan.

CHAPTER 27

Alison reached The Paint and the Pendulum, pulled her sweater over her head like a shield, took a deep breath, and rammed it into the glass of the door. The glass shattered over her back as she ducked inside.

She hobbled along aisles stocked with paint and paint thinners and varnishes. Rummaging through the store, fighting through the pain in her body, she took a screwdriver and began prying lids off cans, piercing the metal containers of varnishes and thinners, dumping them out, creating a noxious colorful river. The fumes were strong, and she tried not to inhale too deeply as she went along dumping more and more liquid from cans.

When she'd reached the end of the aisle, she took the flare from her bra and held it in her hand.

"Come on you little bastard!" she screamed.

The machine was fast. It found her with ease, launching itself right into the store, busting through a window that shattered all around it. The bot knocked aside a display of paint cans, rolling right into the flammable river.

Chopping Mall

Hiding behind a shelving unit, Alison smiled. The Protector had played right into her hands, and it wasn't going anywhere.

Alison quietly ducked out the way she came in. All the while, she never let her eyes stray from the robot, fearing it would have some new secret weapon to set itself free.

She popped the safety cap, a wicked sneer on her face.

"HEY!" she said.

The killer bot lifted its head and regarded her, almost pitifully.

"Have a nice day!"

She flung the flare into the store like a grenade, a perfect pitch that landed at the machine's treads. There was a split-second delay in the detonation. But when it came, the whole store went black. A cloud of smoke roiled and blew open the whole storefront with a wall of rolling flames. Alison was blown back off her feet. She landed hard, and everything went black.

* * *

Sometime later, Alison struggled to open her eyes. She was somewhere on her belly, pain radiating through her body. The heat of the store was on her like a summer sun. Straining to look over her shoulder, she saw the place gutted with flames and smoke. And something else…

The Protector. It was in there, ripped apart and disabled; a skeletal framework of steel crawling with flames, its head broken at the neck, spitting sparks.

It was time to go. To get out of this nightmare mall, this…*chopping* mall, she thought darkly. If she had to crawl out of there, she would. But she fought the pain and got to her knee, then to her feet, gritting her teeth. It was no easy feat. It felt like her whole body had been spit out of a wood-chipper and put together all wrong. She struggled to stand. But she would, and she would beat those mall doors open if that's what she had to do.

"*Hey,*" a soft voice said from above.

Her gaze went to the second level.

She had never wanted to cry so badly in her life. Tears were stinging her eyes. Ferdy was up there, leaning over the rail, smiling down at her like some angel. He was holding a rag to his head, his smile open and beautiful as ever.

"Nice shot," he said.

Teras streamed down her face without end. She could not believe she was seeing him.

Ferdy ran down the escalator. Bounding three steps at a time. He rushed over to her, carefully wrapping his arms around her.

"We made it. We're going to be okay," he said.

She fell into him without a word, her hands pressed tightly into his back. She never wanted to let go.

EPILOGUE
PROTECTOR 2.0

There was so much to clean up...so much to *cover* up. Quickly.

Not only was speed of the essence, but efficiency. Body bags were slapped out and stuffed with the remains. Not an easy beat for the men assigned such grim tasks. Some of the bodies were so beyond composure that the men had to peel or scrape pieces of them off the ground.

"Such a goddamn mess," Colonel Luke Steele commented, shaking his head. His black beret pulled down tight, his jungle fatigues out of line with his surroundings in the Park Plaza Mall. He was addressing Dr. Stan Simon. "You told me these things could withstand anything thrown against them."

The moment he'd received the call that morning, Dr. Simon's mood went south. His salesman demeanor took a backseat as he observed the scene taking place around him, the technicians in their white suits scrambling to sterilize the mall.

"They were designed to be durable and deadly, Colonel," Dr. Simon said. "That's what we discussed. Not impervious to destruction."

Colonel Steele pointed to the crate containing the remains of

Protector 101, its lid nailed shut. "I sure as hell didn't expect it to be broken so easily!"

Dr. Simon had an idea what had gone wrong. Last night's storm. It must have set the Protectors off. This could jeopardize the entire program.

This program—funded by the Defense Department and led by one Colonel Steele of the United States Army Special Weapons Division—was supposed to be a test run. Dropping three of the latest prototypes into action against hundreds of shoppers would prove their targeting capabilities. Ultimately, the goal was for the Protector units to serve as replacements for the surgical military strike normally handled by human soldiers.

Now, with the mission compromised, they had to hurry and erase any sign of the Protectors' involvement and subsequent malfunction—completely eradicating any evidence of anyone's presence in the melee.

"Your goddamn machines couldn't withstand a freak storm—not to mention a group of mall employees!" He wrung his hands in the air. "*Teenagers*, for God's sake! Lord knows what would have happened if those things faced off against *real* targets!"

"These were just prototypes, Colonel. A new wave of killer machines, but untested. You understood there was no guarantee."

Millions of dollars had been poured into the operation only to result in three Protector units completely destroyed. One little storm busting it all up.

"You know what this means, right?" Steele asked.

Dr. Simon nodded. "Sure, you'll have to go in front of the Council again, explain the situation to them."

"And you think that'll be easy?"

"Not at all. But I think you're letting your emotions control the situation right now."

Steele's face went red. "Of course I'm letting my goddamn emotions control me! Look at this mess!"

"You're not thinking, Steele." Simon's grin was impish and cryptic. "You don't have to inform the Council about this little boo-boo."

Steele set his hands on his hips. "What are you getting at?"

"I mean, we're cleaning this place up. Nobody outside knows a thing." Simon's technicians had arrived ahead of any mall employees. With the help of Steele's soldiers, they had locked the place down and pulled any existing security footage.

Steele saw where this was going and his demeanor changed. "That's a fine point, Simon."

Dr. Simon knew it was. "And don't forget, Colonel, there's always Protector 2.0..."

* * *

Undisclosed Testing Facility,
Southern California.
Log No. 0345

Alarms were ringing, red lights strobing.

Screams echoed through the facility, along with the wet cracking of bones being ripped from bodies. Blood splashed down corridors, automatic weapons fire fell silent.

Dr. Carol Vanders knew it was coming for her. Her blue eyes pinned open wide, sweat on her face, blonde hair in a bun, she was the last one in the facility alive.

Earlier, she and Dr. Thompson had been going about their daily routine when suddenly The Protector 2.0 robot had burst through its glass shell, clamped its metal hand around Dr. Thompson's neck and ripped his head right off. The rogue robot then proceeded to rip the heads off of everyone else in the room.

Everyone but Dr. Vanders.

She'd ducked out of the room as a handful of frantic soldiers rushed in, their weapons crackling. Vanders watched the towering machine go to each man in a jerking, mechanical motion and pull them inside out, bathing in their blood, its eyes electric-red.

The Protector approached the final soldier, its eyes glowing hot. It sent its arm down the man's throat, groping in his belly and taking hold.

Vanders paled as she watched the machine pull the soldier inside out. The man looked down at the Protector's arm as it slipped out of his mouth with a handful of meat and blood. He collapsed like an empty sack.

Then the Protector's laser beam gaze turned to her. She instantly ran screaming.

But there was no escaping Protector 2.0. It was a hunter, a night-stalker, a *perfect* terminator. It caught up to her, took her by the bun of her hair, and hoisted her off the ground. Finally, it ripped off her scalp and shoved it into her mouth. Dr. Carol Vanders' screams muffled as the Protector rammed its cold metal fingers into her eye sockets, then ripped her face open. Brains and blood glopped to the floor. It dropped what was left of her.

The Protector sat very still. It registered a new sound. Somewhere outside the facility, the footfalls of more soldiers could be heard approaching the facility.

Protector 2.0 was ready for them. It was the *perfect* killing machine. There would be no stopping it.

The following pages feature images from the film *Chopping Mall*. Used by permission.

CHOPPING MALL

Where Shopping Costs You an Arm and a Leg!

STARRING
KELLI MARONEY
TONY O'DELL · JOHN TERLESKY
RUSSEL TODD PAUL BARTEL
MARY WORONOV AND DICK MILLER

WRITTEN BY
JIM WYNORSKI & STEVE MITCHELL

ROBOTS CREATED BY
ROBERT SHORT

PRODUCED BY
JULIE CORMAN

DIRECTED BY
JIM WYNORSKI

R RESTRICTED
UNDER 17 REQUIRES ACCOMPANYING
PARENT OR ADULT GUARDIAN

1986 CONCORDE/TRINITY PICTURES

BUY OR DIE...

CHOPPING MALL

M FOR MATURE AUDIENCES

Where shopping costs you an arm and a leg!

Starring **RUSSEL TODD** (FRIDAY THE 13TH), **BARBARA CRAMPTON** (RE-ANIMATOR), **KELLI MARONEY** (NIGHT OF THE COMET) and **TONY O'DELL** (THE KARATE KID).

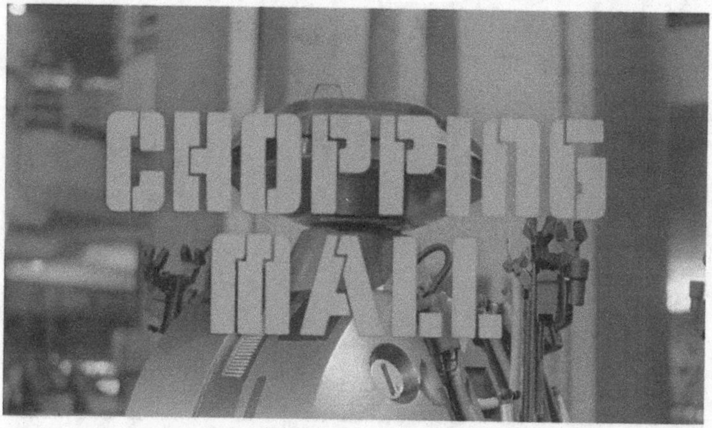
CHOPPING
MALL

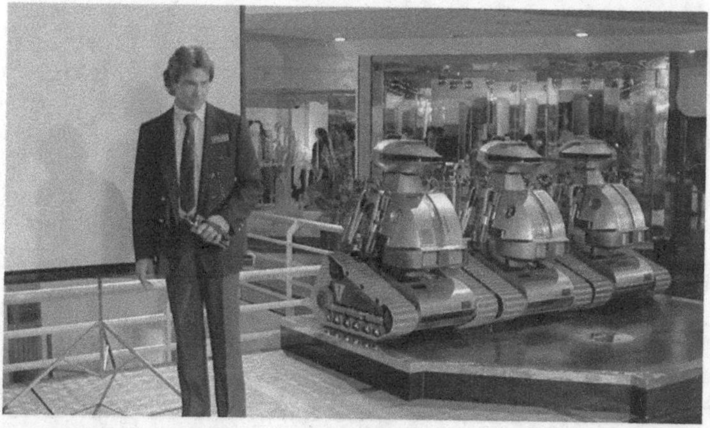

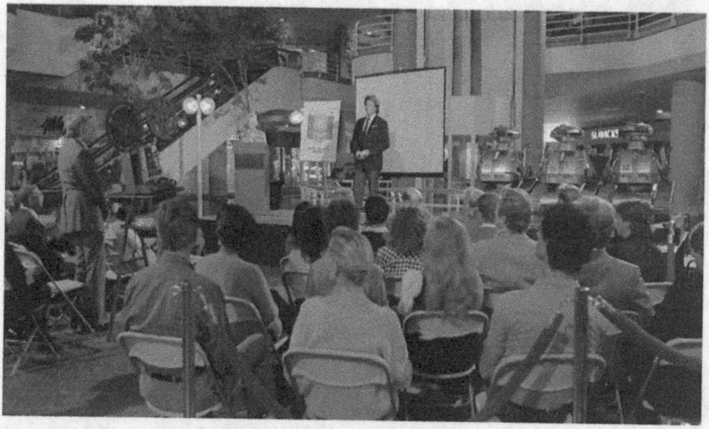

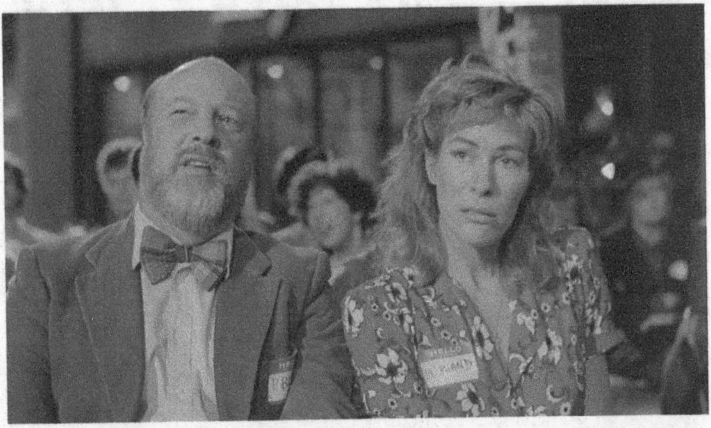

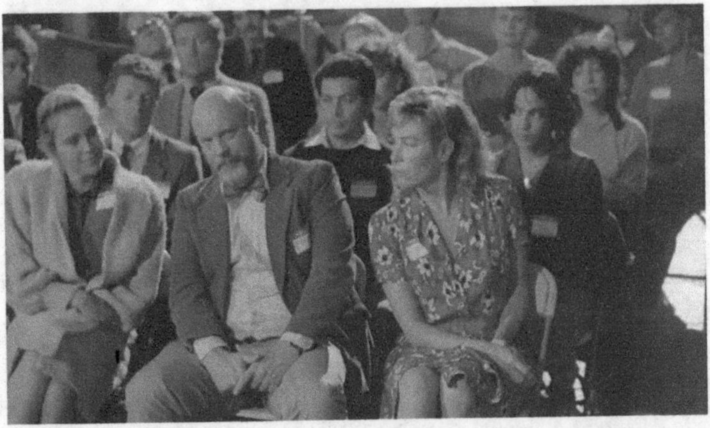

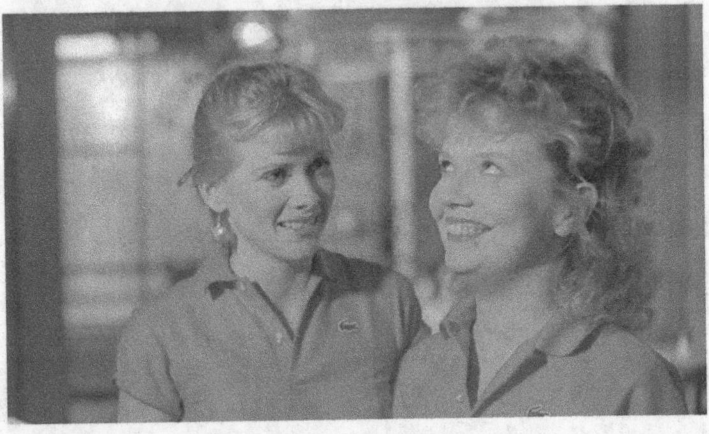

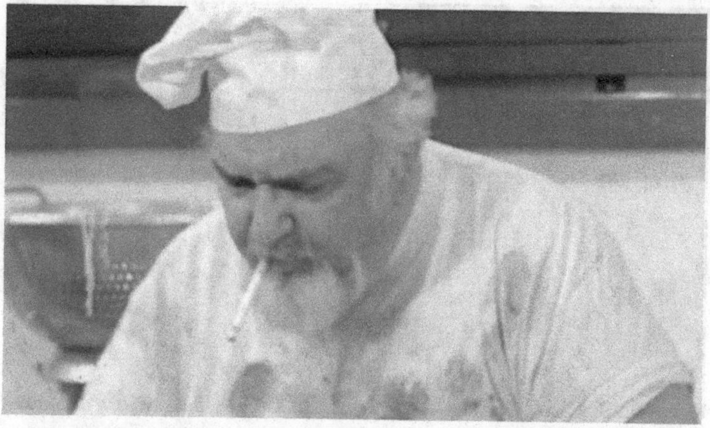

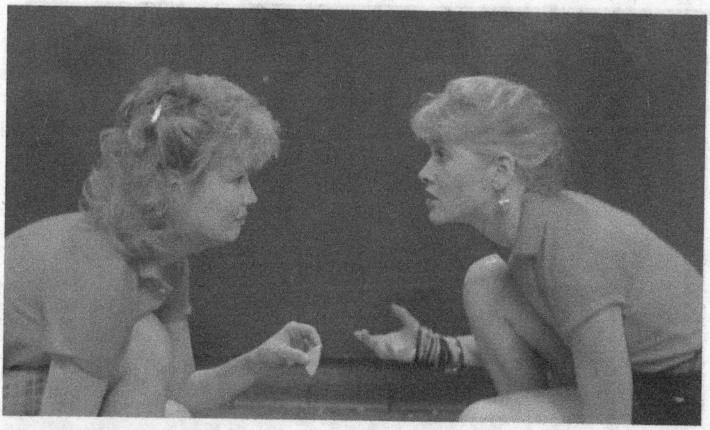

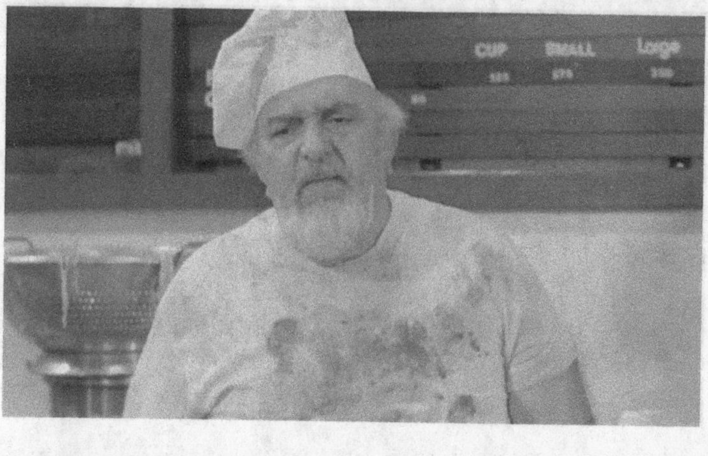
CUP
SMALL
Large

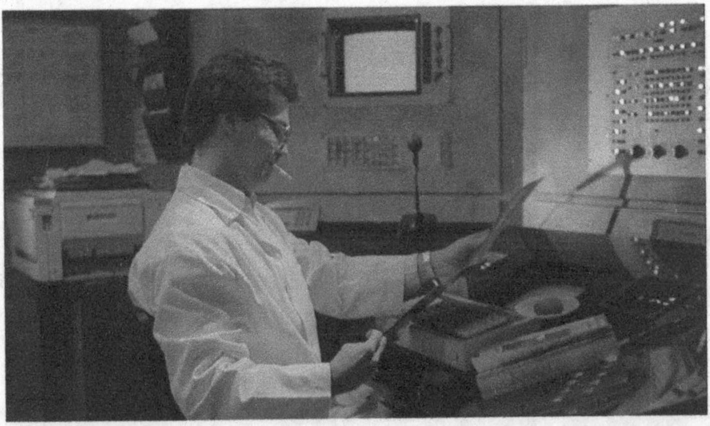

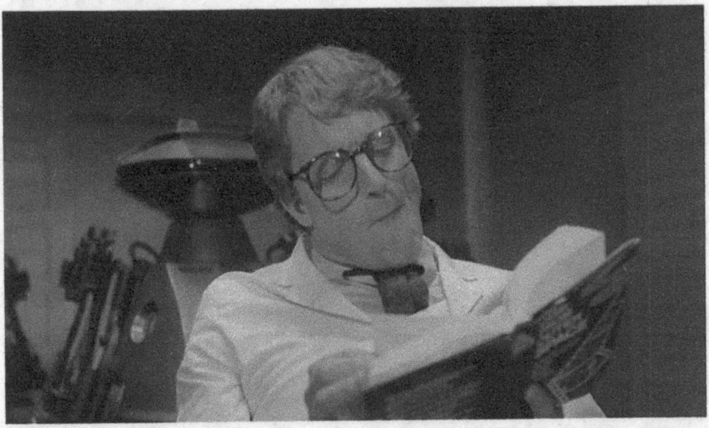

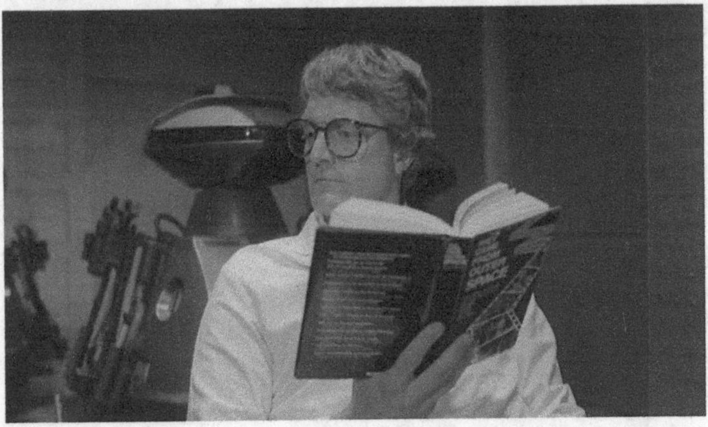

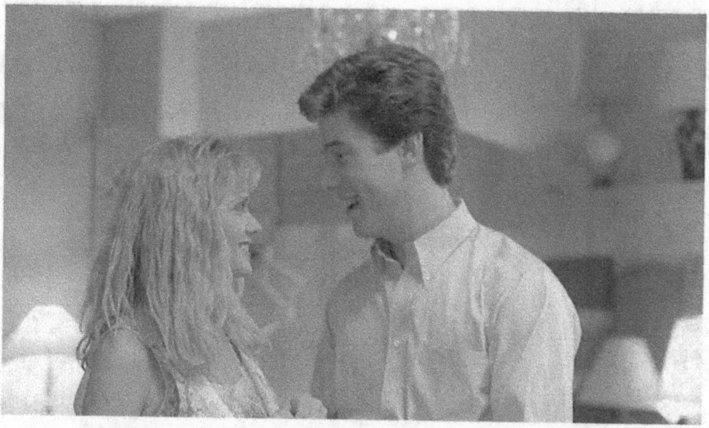

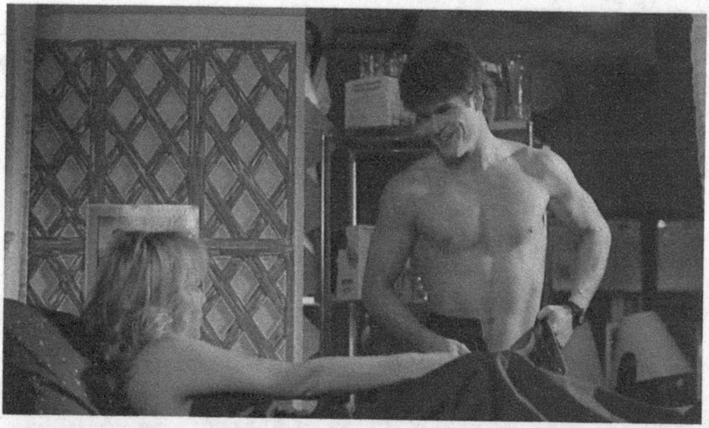

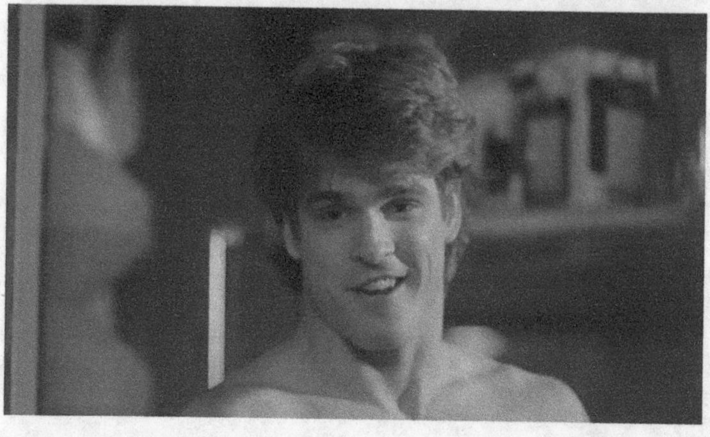

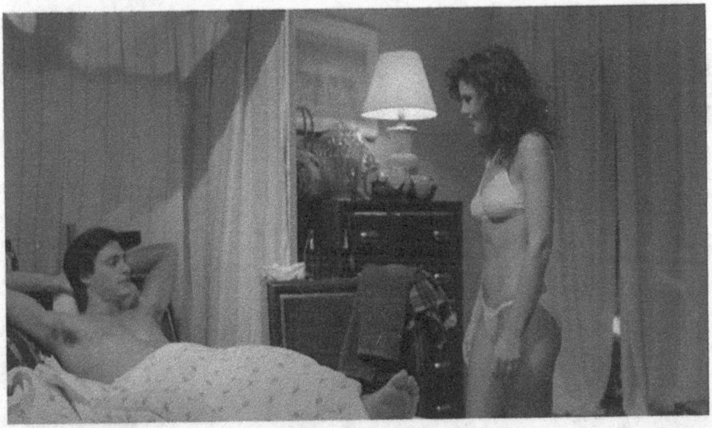

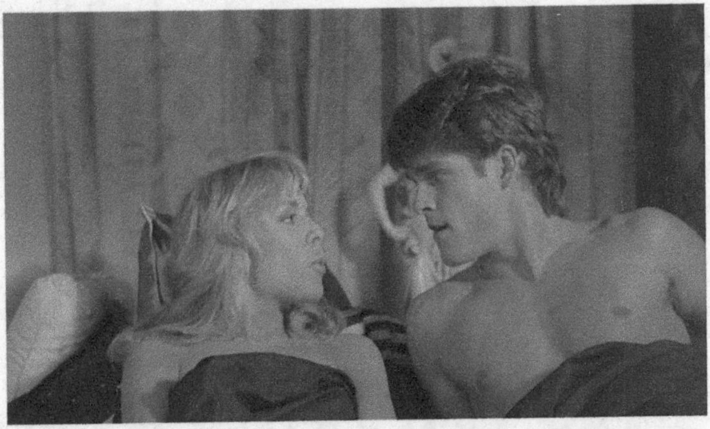

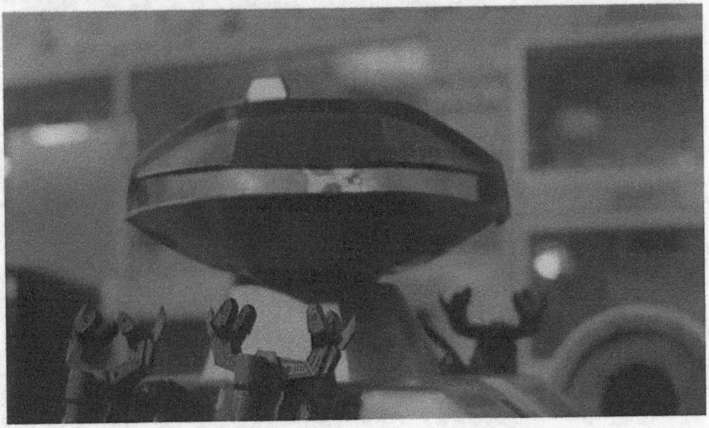

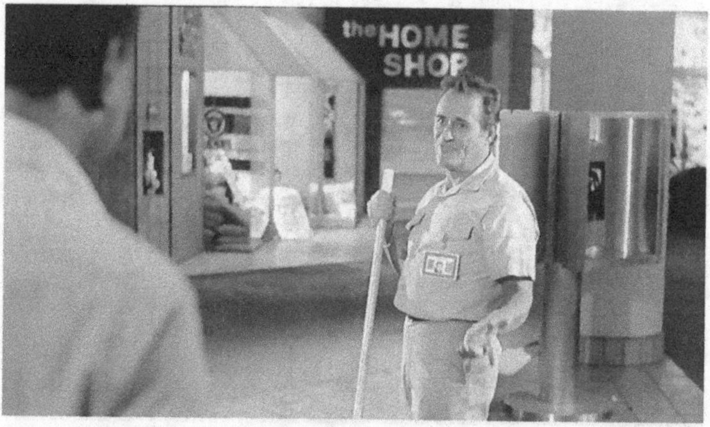
the HOME
SHOP

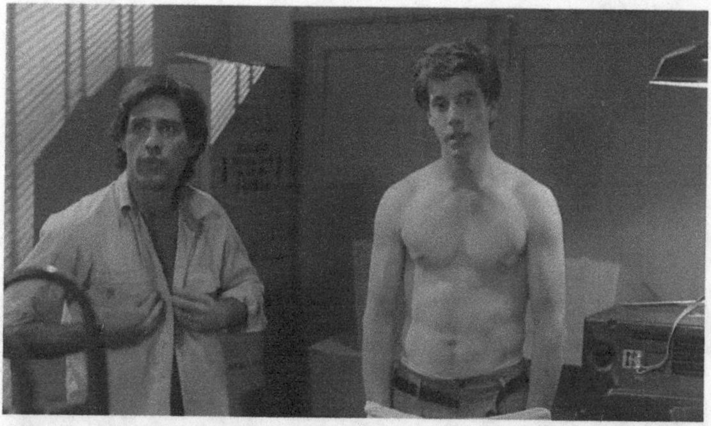

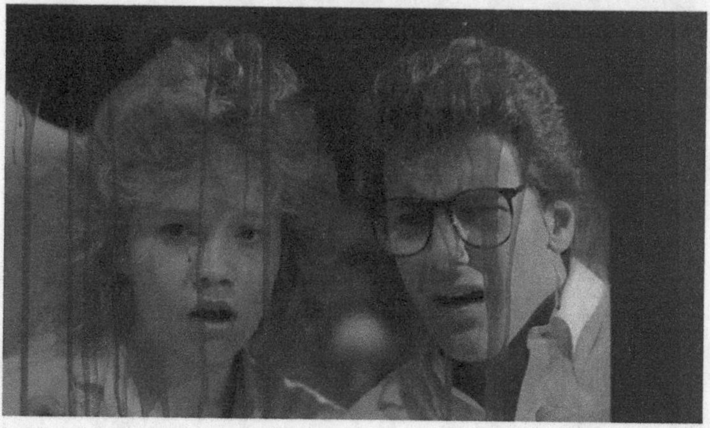

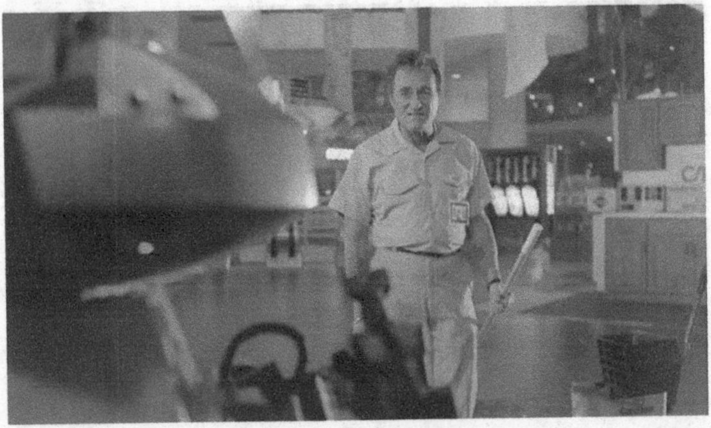

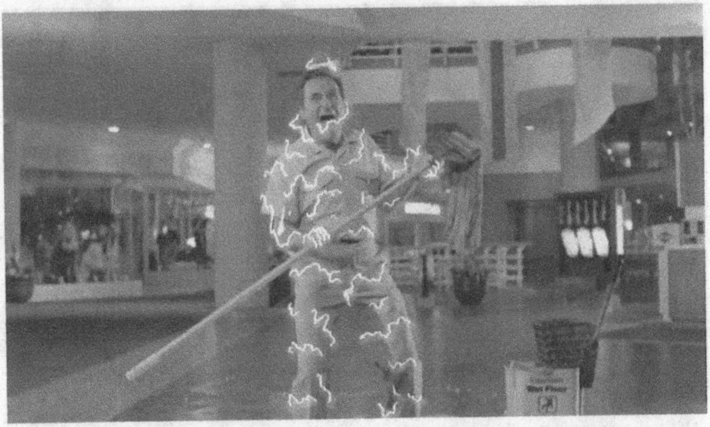

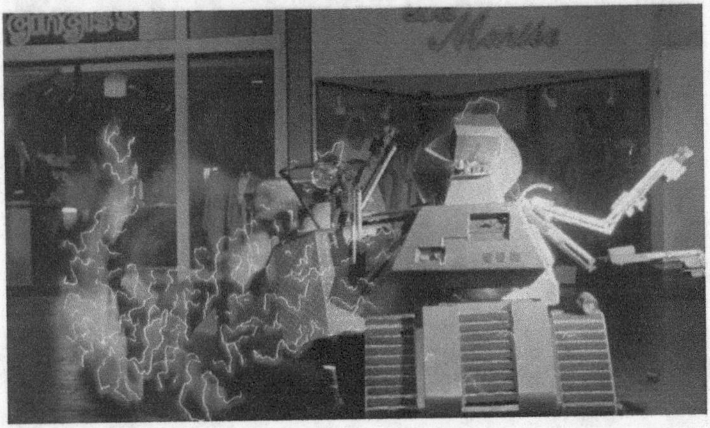

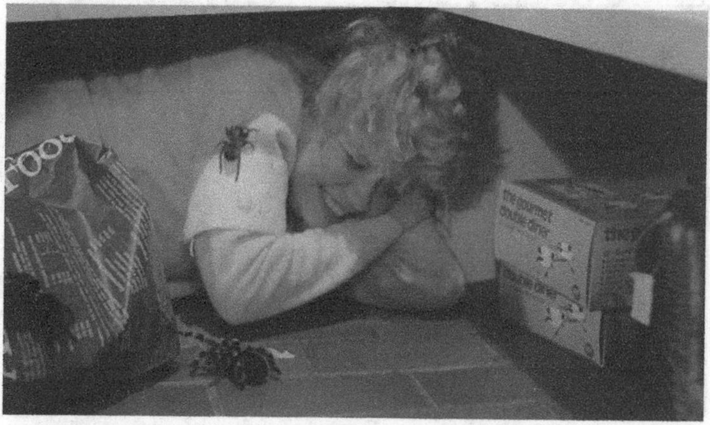

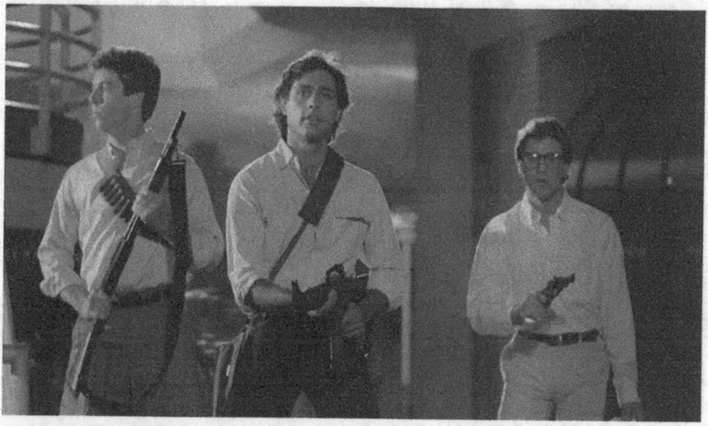

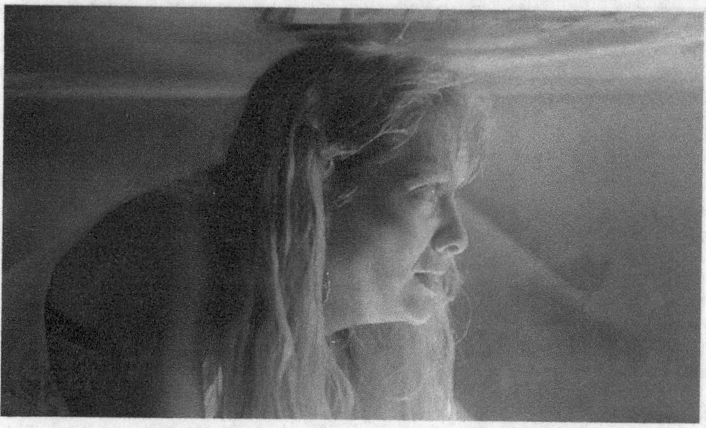

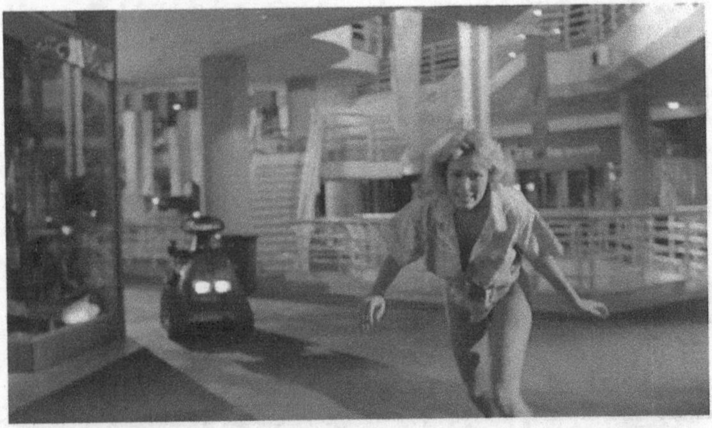

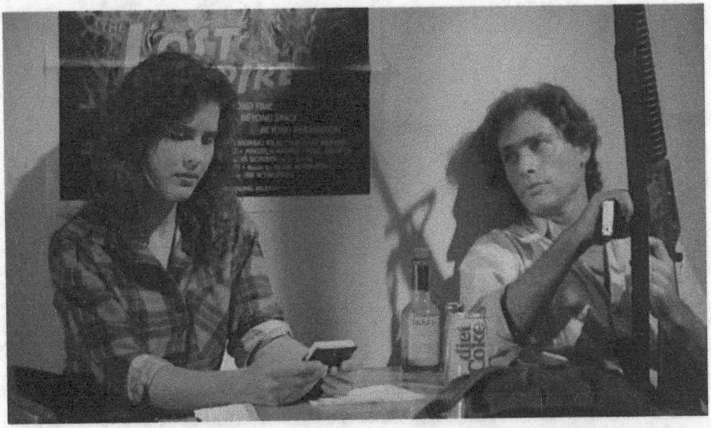
diet Coke

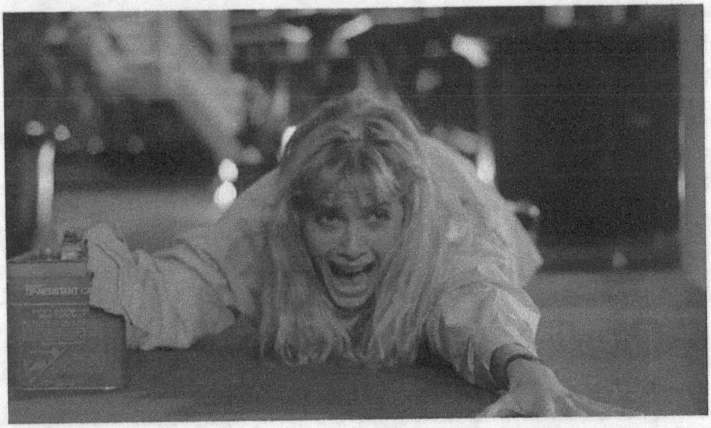

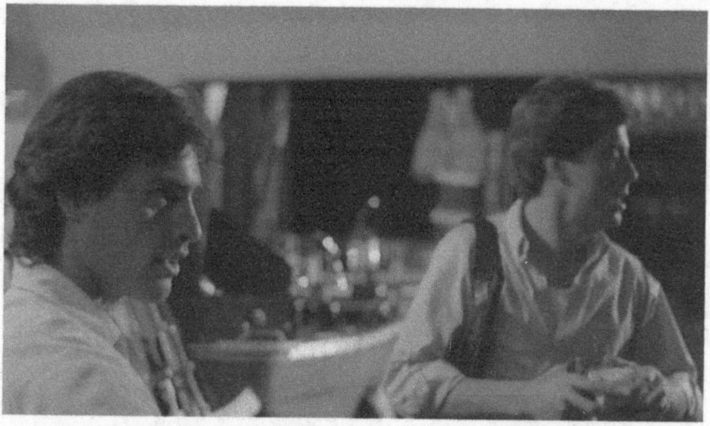

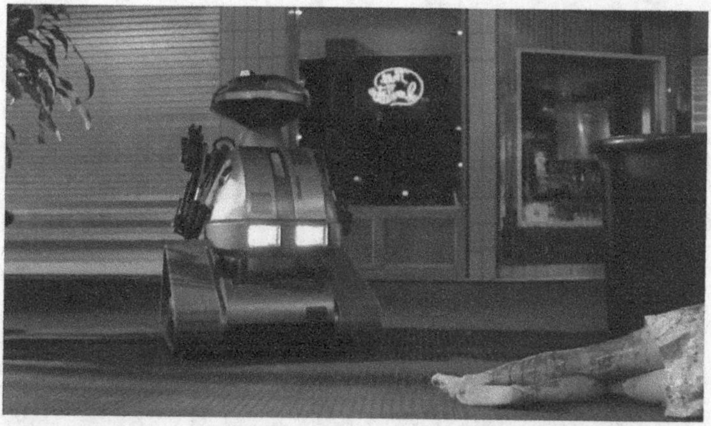

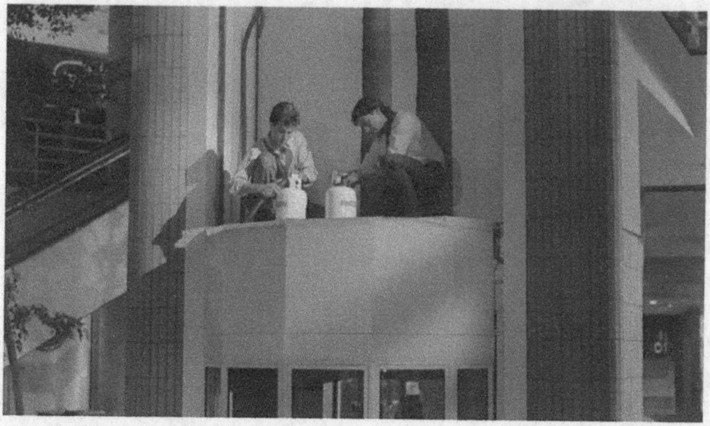

ABOUT THE AUTHOR

Brian G Berry is the author of over fifty novels, ranging from horror, to action, and science fiction. A few of his more popular book titles are as follows: Snow Shark, Sleepover Massacre, Blood Feast of the Ghoul God, Sharpshooter Terror, and Rapid Madness. When he's not writing, he's publishing anthologies/authors with his company Slaughterhouse Press.